I'M JUST TRYIN' TO BE SOMEBODY'S WIFE

COLE HART

Mailing List

To stay up to date on new releases, plus get information on contests, sneak peeks, and more,

Go To The Website Below...

www.colehartsignature.com

We make plans, and God laughs.

CHAPTER 1

*I*t was only the first day of summer and the drama had already started in Augusta. A black Tundra pickup truck pulled up in the front of Walmart on Deans Bridge road, coming to a screeching halt at the exit. There was a young girl driving, looking to be no older than eighteen, but she was almost twenty-one. She had her left hand on the steering wheel, holding her iPhone 8 in her right hand with it on speaker.

"I'm outside yo' job right now, bitch." She growled into the phone with a sinister smile on her face. Nu Nu was the name that she went by; she was a dark chocolate female with a well-shaped body; her waist was tight and her backside sported a healthy roundness that tapered down to slim thick thighs. You can tell she worked out. Nu Nu had hood chick and project drama queen written all over her face, and she was always into something. A real ill-tempered little girl with low and high self-esteem, if that made any sense to have both.

"Okay, stay yo' lil dumb ass right there until I get out there," the other female's voice yelled back from the other end.

"Oh, I'm out here, bitch." Nu Nu slammed the truck into park, and not even thinking at the moment, she parked right there in front of the crosswalk. There was a black and gray Richmond County police car parked three feet away from her that she didn't see. She opened the door, stepped down from the truck. A lady was walking in front of her truck pushing a grocery cart, looking at Nu Nu as if she was crazy. When she noticed how the lady was staring at her, she stared back and said, "You lost sumt'?"

The lady turned her head away from her and kept it moving. Then out of the blue, a deep voice yelled out, "Hey lady, move the truck."

Nu Nu spun around with a frown on her face, and just when she was about to let her reckless mouth fly off the handle, she noticed that it was the police talking to her. Her entire demeanor changed; she eased her phone in her left side back pocket. Then she said to herself, *Damn, let me get out of here. I forgot about the shoplifting warrant I have.* She smiled, throwing her hand up in the air. "Yes sir, sorry about that." And soon as she turned around, there was another Sheriff car pulling up; the officer was black and had his driver side window down, appearing to just be making a routine check. When he stopped the car, his eyes were dead on her.

"Oh, Nu Nu," he said, like he knew her.

"Hey, I was just leavin', sir," she said, and opened the driver side door; without another word from the officer, he watched her hop into the front seat. The truck was still running, while she pulled her seatbelt across her and clicked it in. She closed the door, looked at him, and pulled out the parking lot like she had some sense. With both hands on the wheel and checking her rearview mirror, she cruised across the parking lot. The night was still young to her. When she got out of Walmart parking lot, she reached in her back pocket and grabbed her phone and dialed the girl's number that was inside of Walmart. She allowed the phone to ring several times before it went to the voicemail. Nu Nu laughed and left her a message on her voice mail. "**Look bitch, you got me out here losin' my cool about YO NIGGA. And the only reason I'm gonna beat yo ass cause YO NIGGA got some good dick.**" She laughed at her comment and hung up the phone.

* * *

INSIDE THE WALMART STORE, THERE WAS A YOUNG LADY standing at the front entrance named Asia. She was twenty-one years old and had been working at Walmart a little under a year. Asia was knock-out beautiful, possessing thin pouty lips, high cheekbones, and slanted eyes. With a well-shaped body and evenly toned yellow skin, Asia wasn't a hood chick or anything, and she wasn't born in Augusta. Her father was in the military at Fort Gordon, and her mother lived out on base. Even though they were separated, Asia decided to get out on her own. She had big plans for her future. But the way things were going now with all this drama that her boyfriend Sean was bringing into her life, she was baffled. She held her iPhone up to her face while she listened to the message that Nu Nu had just left. Asia was nearly in tears; she couldn't even believe what she was hearing at the moment.

She dialed Sean's number. Da Baby was playing as his ring tone. She used to like the song, but now since all this was going on, she hated it.

"What up baby?" Sean asked from the other end.

Asia frowned. "What up baby?" she said in a tone of voice as if she couldn't believe what she was hearing. "Bra, you got this bitch coming up to my job trying to fight, you got *MY CAR*, and you late on picking me, and all you can say is what up baby?"

"What? Who came to yo' job?" he asked from the other end.

"Sean, don't play crazy with me," she told him, desperately fighting back her tears. "Are you coming to get me or what?" Her eyes were tearing up; she didn't want none of her

3

coworkers to see her and the embarrassing look that she had on her face.

"Check game, baby, I'm over here in Aiken, South Carolina 'bout to pick up this work. Trust me on this, go ahead and catch an Uber. By the time you get…"

"An Uber? Really nigga, are you serious right now?" she nearly yelled into the phone, and then looked around to see if anyone was looking at her. Asia took a long deep breath, lifting her bag across her right shoulder. She headed towards the door, they parted automatically, and as she was walking outside, Sean's voice came through the phone.

"So, I'm askin' too much from you right now?"

Asia couldn't believe what she was hearing; she rolled her eyes and shook her head from side to side. Then in a low voice, she said into the phone, "Okay, I'll see you later." She ended the call and walked out in front of the store. It was night and the temperature felt like a smooth warm seventy-five degrees with a light breeze blowing. Asia walked across the parking lot toward Popeye's restaurant. She didn't want her coworkers to know what she had going on, so she called for the Uber driver to pick her up there. Her steps were casual, and she had a lot on her mind; especially with a situation like that. In her mind, she was finished with Sean. *This dumb ass girl actually came to my job trying to fight,* she thought, and shook her head in disgust.

When Asia walked inside Popeye's, the fried chicken aroma hit her nose. It smelled good, but she didn't have an appetite whatsoever. She walked over to one of the booths and grabbed a seat. She unlocked her iPhone and looked at the screen. She then called her best friend on Facetime. She listened to the light sound of the ringing as she looked at her reflection in the phone screen.

No answer.

Sucking her teeth, she looked at the time on her phone. It was ten minutes after ten. Asia's emotions were all over the place; she was thinking about everything. And her boyfriend was too nonchalant about the whole situation. Her phone suddenly rang. Looking at the screen, the name Imani was splashed across the display. She answered.

"Girl, don't be ignoring my calls."

"Come on friend, you already know we don't do that. Where you at?" Imani asked from the other end.

"Just got off, now I'm sitting here in Popeye's waiting for an Uber."

"An Uber? Let me guess, Sean got your car again..."

"Tuh, and not only that, his side chick pulled up on me at my job. This bitch actually got my number, called me, and came out here." She rolled her eyes at the thought of it.

"The fuck?" Imani shouted from the other end. "Best friend, I keep telling you to leave that nigga alone. All that childish ass hood shit. You too good and pretty for that dude. Do you want me to come get you?"

"I'm good, my Uber will be here in a minute. I'm just trying to figure out how to get out of this situation." She held up the phone and lowered her eyes.

"Girl, you just gotta leave."

Asia was quiet when she heard that. She wanted to get away from him indefinitely; she wasn't used to this type of life.

"Are you there?" Imani asked from the other end.

She snapped out of her thoughts; her eyes went to the phone. "I'm here," she said in a whispered tone, feeling the tears pushing from the back of her eyes. And when she took a deep breath, she saw a guy walk in through the door where she was sitting. She made eye contact with him as he had his eyes dead on her for some apparent reason. *Maybe he's the Uber driver,* she thought before saying into the phone, "Let me call you back, Imani." Ending the call, she aptly watched the guy that was now at the counter with his back to her. Here she was, sitting there in a Walmart uniform, her hair was not looking its best from her sweating, and she was tired and mentally drained. And she was checking out a guy that she had never seen before.

He turned around, faced her, and casually walked toward her. Asia dropped her head and pretended to be looking at her phone, but it was too late. He made it to her, stopping in front of her. He placed his hand out in front of her. She noticed his long chocolate fingers first. His nails were clean and trimmed. But what really caught her eye was the gold Audemars Piguet watch with a diamond bezel. When Asia finally looked up at him, he was looking down at her. "I'm just tryin' to introduce myself," he said in a deep southern accent.

Asia smiled, placing her tiny hand in his and feeling his strength. "Hello," she finally said. She started examining him, noticing that he wasn't that tall. Just right at five nine or ten at the most, but he had wide shoulders, like a running back. His skin complexion was a mid-brown, nearly the same color as a paper bag.

"I'm Asia, and I actually have to leave because my Uber just pulled up." She stood to her feet, just a compact five foot four inches.

"Asia, cool name." He was still holding her hand and smiling at her.

"Thanks, and what's yours?" she asked.

"They call me Big Tex when I'm not in Texas. But you can call me Angelo."

"And Angelo is your real name?" she asked with a smile.

He let her hand go, reached in his back pocket to pull out his wallet. As soon as she noticed it, she quickly stopped him.

"I believe you." She started moving toward the door. "I don't want this Uber to leave me."

"Cool, I'll walk you outside." Then he stepped back and allowed her to lead the way. As they were headed out of the door, he said. "Shoot me your info or I'll give you mines." He opened the door for her, and she walked outside and saw the Uber driver sitting there waiting for her in a white Jetta.

The driver rolled her window down and smiled at her. "You still need the Uber?" she asked her.

"Yes, I'm on the way. One second," Asia said to her and turned and faced the stranger that stood in front of her. She pulled out her iPhone and handed it to him. "Put your number in," she said cheerfully.

He took her phone and punched in one of his three cell numbers that he had. When he pulled his phone out and looked at, he held it up to her face. "That's you?"

"Yes," she told him, then she turned around and headed toward the lady that was waiting for her. She looked back at him. "Nice to meet you, Angelo." She went around to the passenger side and got in. He'd already turned around and was heading back inside Popeye's.

CHAPTER 2

*a*sia got in the front seat with the lady that was driving the Uber; she closed the door and looked at her with a smile. "I'm sorry for having you waiting," she said.

"It's alright," she said back to Asia. For the next twenty minutes, Asia rode in silence and strolled Instagram on her way home. She had a thing for watching quotes and motivation and things of that sort. Asia's mind was moving in twenty different directions. It went back to her boyfriend Sean; he was dirty as hell for not picking her up from work. But apparently, she liked it because she was allowing it to happen over and over again. Then she thought about the situation with the hood rat Nu Nu. *The nerve of that bitch,* she thought.

The Uber driver pulled up to her apartment building and she got out. The loud smell of lit marijuana was in the air. Asia was one of those type of girls that lived in an apartment complex that didn't talk to anyone there and wasn't interested in meeting any new friends. There was a small mixed crowd of men and women huddled around a Yukon SUV. They appeared to be just listening to music, smoking, drinking, and having fun. Asia lived on the first floor in building C, apartment 230. When she got inside, she locked her door, flipping on the light switch to her front room. She had her cozy apartment tastefully decorated with a three-piece brown leather sofa set, a brass and glass coffee table, and a seventy-inch smart TV mounted on her wall. She went down the hall that led to the only bedroom in the apartment. Asia began taking off her work clothes to get comfortable. She sat on the side of her bed and kicked off her shoes before she dialed Sean's number from her iPhone, trying to Facetime him. After it rung several times and he didn't answer, she hung it up and tried to dial it again.

Nothing.

"Well, I already know he cheatin'.... so, I'll just chalk it up," she whispered. Getting up to go to the bathroom, her phone rang. She paused, turned around, and headed back toward the bed where her phone was. It was Sean calling back. She answered. "Where are you, Sean?" she asked, her face turned into a frown, but it was more of a disgusted look. She was staring at the floor as she listened to him.

"Shawty, you ain't gon' believe this," he said. Then he went on with what he started. "Man, I had a small delay, it'll be a couple of hours before I get home."

Asia took a deep breath and began shaking her head side to side as she took in his lies and tried to swallow them like a tough piece of steak. She rubbed her hand across her face and forehead. Then she finally said into her iPhone, "Okay, whatever, Sean." She hung up in his face. Just ending the call, tears began to fall from her eyes, and she laid back on her bed for the next few minutes and cried uncontrollably.

After a few minutes, she just laid there and stared at the ceiling, her favorite Teddy bear wrapped up in her arms. Her phone chimed, and she slowly picked it up and looked at the screen; it was an alert message on Instagram from her friend Imani. She opened it up and it read: **Hey friend, I saw this floating around on Social media and thought about you.**

. . .

BLOCK THAT NIGGA AND LET LIL UGLY HAVE HIM.

ASIA COULDN'T DO ANYTHING BUT SMILE AT THAT MEME, THEN she typed and responded back to the message. **If you only knew how much this just cheered me up. Honestly this nigga is stressing me the fuck out. I just wish I could just disappear and get the hell away from Augusta.**

IMANI TYPED BACK: **IF THAT WHAT IT TAKES TO GET THE HELL AWAY from that Clown, you got to do you. I'm about to take a shower and get ready for work. Keep me posted okay.**

ASIA RESPONDED: **OKAY. SEE YOU TOMORROW.** SHE TOSSED HER phone on the bed, got up, and went into the bathroom. After turning on the shower, she looked at herself in the mirror. "You too pretty and too loyal for this nigga," she said to her reflection. The water from the shower was quickly steaming up the mirror. Asia began to undress. Pulling her khaki pants down over her curvy hips, she stepped out of them one leg at a time. Her thighs were thick, and her stomach had a small pouch. When she removed her shirt and bra, she admired herself in the mirror. She had the nicest set of titties that could be made. Asia gathered up her clothes and tossed them into the dirty clothes hamper, got into the hot shower, and relaxed and washed herself. Her mind went back to the guy she'd just met at Popeye's; she thought long and deep about him. He had a grown man presence. Not like Sean. She smiled and tried to push the thoughts away from her mind.

No more than fifteen minutes later, she was dressed in an

over-sized t-shirt and lace panties. She went back into her bedroom, laid across her bed, and strolled IG from her iPhone. Then she took a selfie holding her Teddy bear and posted it on the gram. Her caption read: *Missing him. #LoveSick #InMyFeelings.*

* * *

NO MORE THAN A MINUTE LATER, THE FIRST COMMENT CAME IN under her picture. Asia nearly froze when she read it: **I'm missing him too. And I haven't talked to him all day. He better not be cheating on us.** The post was from Nu Nu. That was it for Asia. She blocked Nu Nu for the third time and then she deactivated her page; she was really angry now. She went to her contacts and called Sean on Facetime, and to her surprise, he answered the call. But at that moment, she saw his sexy green eyes stretched wide. "Shawty, I'm on a high-speed chase," he said with a panicky look in his eyes.

"Why don't you just stop, Sean," she said to him.

"Bitch, is you crazy!" he said. "I'm ridin' dirty as hell. Go ahead and report the car stolen." Then he ended the call.

Asia swallowed and got up. She didn't know what to do at this point. The car was in her mother's name; she couldn't afford for her to be in her business. She got up out the bed, dialed Sean's number again, and it just played Da Baby in her ears. She ended the call and dialed her friend's number. Now, Imani wasn't answering either. Asia began pacing the floor, going from her room to the living room. She peeped out the curtain, but she couldn't see anything. Her heart was racing, and she needed someone to talk to; it was already pass eleven o'clock and she knew her mother was sleep. She went and sat on her sofa, pulled her knees up to her chest, and didn't move for the next twenty minutes. She wasn't about to report her car stolen; she just couldn't do it. Her mother wouldn't let her live it down. She could hear her voice replaying in her head now. *The worst thing you can do is to allow a no good nigga to use you.* And here she was allowing it to happen like her mother hadn't ever said it to her. Asia sat back on the couch, trying to close her eyes and relax for a few minutes. Her thoughts were tugging at her in a way that made her sweat and had her nerves jumping.

Then out of nowhere, she heard keys at the front door. She looked up and then she stood to her feet as Sean was coming through the front door. He was moving like someone was behind him, breathing hard and moving nervously. When he turned around and faced her, he had a smile on his face. He was dressed in skinny jeans, Air Force One Nikes, and a knockoff Dolce & Gabbana t-shirt. Asia was now standing directly in front of him; Sean was only a few inches taller than her.

While he was looking down at her, he noticed the anger and fire that were in her eyes. And before she could say anything, he quickly got down on one knee and went in his front pocket at the same time. When he pulled his hand out, he was holding a velvet ring box. He flipped it open and there was a solid one-carat diamond ring sitting on a mound of rose gold. She was looking down at his sexy green eyes when he said, "Please accept my apology and give me the chance to be your husband." He sounded so good to her, his voice was smooth and deep, and his alluring eyes had her at "hello."

Asia stood there, speechless for a moment, then out of the blue, she drew her arm back, her tiny hand clutched into a tiny fist. When she swung her fist, it connected straight in his right eye. **WHOP!** "Fuck you, nigga," she yelled out as drops of spit flew from her mouth. She then knocked the ring from his hand, and it flew somewhere across the room. "And fuck that ring too." Tears of pure anger were flowing down her face now, and she was breathing like she'd been running for the last twenty minutes. Sean didn't say anything as he touched the side of his face where she'd hit him.

Still, not one word came from his mouth. Then he looked in the direction of where she sent the ring flying across the room, his head moving slowly as if he was a robot. Sean took a long deep breath and looked down at the floor for a moment, he didn't expect this, and now he was actually trying to take it all in. Asia backed away from him; she did what she did but deep down inside, it was all out of anger and frustration.

She moved.

One.

Two.

Three.

And by the time she was on her fourth step, she saw Sean reaching underneath his shirt, his hand seemed to be moving in slow motion. She had her eyes on him. The gun came out. Gripped firmly in his hand, Sean stood to his feet, but he never pointed the gun at Asia. However, she turned and ran into her bedroom and slammed the door behind her.

Asia instantly locked the door. She stood there for a moment, listening before hearing the doorknob turning quickly. That scared her for sure as she thought about a scene similar from a scary movie.

As she backed away from the door, Asia heard Sean say in a calm manner, "Open the door, Asia." The knob twisted loudly.

"Boy, you crazy as hell," she said back.

"Open the door, Asia," Sean calmly said again.

"Sean, you're standing out there with a gun in your hand and you want me to open the door." Her voice was calm as well.

"Asia, you hit me in my motha' fuckin' eye *and* you slapped the ring across the room. And you expect me to act civilized?" He was fuming; his eyes had turned into thin slits. Sean was on the verge of exploding at any moment.

Asia rolled her eyes. "Dude, you got bitches coming to my job trying to fight me, the same bitch stalking me on IG. Talking about *OUR MAN*. You let her get my number and everything. So apparently, you allowed her to go through your phone." She paused for a moment, and then she exhaled a little. "I'm *over* it. I swear on everything I love."

"I did mess up. And I'm not about to sit up here and try to lie to get out of it. But you do know that I love you, bae." Sean was smiling; he was a charmer at some point. But his depression was turning into pure anger by the seconds. He began singing a verse from a Chris Brown song. "I don't wanna play no games, play no games. Fuck around and give you my last name."

Asia fell silent, briefly closing her eyes. Her mother's words came to her again, and at that moment, she knew that she wasn't about to fall for it again. "I need some time to myself, Sean," she finally said.

"Asia, I swear to God! If you don't open this door, I'm going to kill myself right here in yo' livin' room." Sean's words went through the door and seeped into Asia's ears; she couldn't believe what she was hearing.

Her entire mood changed; her face twisted up into a frown. "Man, get the fuck out my house with all the stupid ass shit!" She was furious now, not just because of the situation, but because of the type of conversation he had going on. In the next fifteen seconds, everything became quiet as a mouse. Her heart was beating rapidly as she just stood there listening to it.

KAAAAA BOOM…

The gun roared from the other side of the door. Asia jumped back; she was frightened, her eyes stretching wider than a half a dollar coin. Then, another loud roaring gunshot rang out.

KAAAA BOOM…

But it was something different about that sound; it seemed as if it was coming through the wood. Asia looked down at the door and noticed that the bullets were coming through the door and into her room.

Sean yelled out, "Bitch, didn't I tell you that I wasn't nothin' to play with." As he sent another bullet through the door, it ripped through the sheetrock wall and her headboard.

Asia ran across the room and headed toward the window, really scared for her life now. She didn't hesitate at all flipping the latch on the window lock. She struggled to raise it up, but her adrenaline wasn't about to let her down.

Sean was busting through the door now, getting into the room. His Glock 19 was clutched in his hand, but he had it resting against the side of his thigh. His eyes were wide as they searched the room. When he finally set his eyes on the window and noticed that the screen had been pushed out, he smiled and walked over to the window, tucking his gun in his back pocket and peeping his head out. When he didn't see her, he quickly turned around and went back to the living room. He stood in the middle of the floor, and then looked in the direction of where the ring could be. He walked over toward the dining room table, scanning the floor left and right, but he didn't find the ring. Sean quickly grabbed a hold of himself. He finally moved his gun from his back pocket and tucked it in his waist, trying his best to pull his shirt down over it. Then he headed toward the front door and walked out into the breezeway. Some of the neighbors in the apartment complex were already standing outside, trying to see what was going on. Sean moved casually, as if he didn't have a clue as to what was going on as well. Sweat was dripping from his face and pores, but the cool night breeze was relaxing him a little.

To his right, an older lady was coming out of the apartment, just next to Asia's apartment. Sean looked at her, she had a painful look on her face, and she was pouring sweat. "Sir, can you please help me," she asked him as he was passing by.

Sean paused for a brief moment and looked at her. "What's wrong?" he asked.

She moved her hand from her right hip and there was a bleeding wound, a bullet hole to be exact. "Someone shot me. I think the bullet came through the window or the wall," she said as the pain was racing through her body. "Just call the police and an ambulance for me," she begged him.

Sean nodded his head. He pulled out his iPhone and started to walk off as he pretended to call the police. When he got to the parking lot, there were several people outside now. Men, women, and even some kids were out trying to see what in the hell was going on. Nothing like this ever happened in their complex before. Sean walked straight passed everyone and then he looked around to see if he could Asia anywhere.

He didn't. Quickly, he left the scene on foot and cut through some bushes that took him to the rear of a Circle K gas station.

CHAPTER 3

A little less than an hour later, the apartment complex was crawling with Richmond County police and detectives. There were two ambulances now and of course, Channel 12 News team was on the scene. Asia was sitting in the rear of one the ambulances with a uniform officer and one of the paramedics. The officer was a black guy with a smooth hairless face and keen eyes. He was sitting in front of Asia with his iPad in his hands and taking notes. When he looked back up at Asia, he noticed that she was shaking nervously; she was wrapped in a blanket and hugging herself. And her eyes were giving off nothing but pure pain and fear. "Now, did he actually tell you that he was going to kill you, or did he just start shooting," the officer asked in a deep and hard tone of voice.

"No, you've already asked me that. He said he was going to kill himself if I didn't open the door. And when I didn't open the door, that's when I heard the gun go off. I thought he'd shot himself until another shot came through the door. After that, I turned and went through the window and ran down the street and hid behind the dumpsters."

The officer began writing something down on his iPad, taking notes very carefully. Then he flipped the iPad towards Asia and held it in front of her. "Is this Sean Murry? The one that was shooting at you," he asked her.

Asia couldn't lie, at this point, she was terrified for her life and was willing to do anything that she could do to get as far away from him as possible. When she looked down at his mugshot, she noticed the small grimace smile on his face. "Yes, that's him," she finally said, and batted her eyes closed.

"Okay great, and you are aware that in the mist of him trying to shoot you, he shot an elderly lady that lives next door?"

Asia's eyes widened with fear. "Oh my God, are you serious? Is she alright?" she asked with genuine concern in her voice; her eyes teared up even more. The female paramedic that was also in the back of the ambulance with her eased her arm around Asia's neck.

"Yes darling, she's fine," she told her, not waiting for the officer to answer the question. "The other ambulance just took her to the hospital. She was shot in her thigh, but she's definitely going to be alright."

Asia couldn't do anything but shake her head from side to side. Closing her eyes, she asked herself, *What have you gotten yourself into?* When she opened her eyes, she was looking directly at the officer that was in front of her. "So, what's next? I'm tired. I need to go to work in the morning, but I'm not sure about that either until you at least catch him."

"And where do you work at," he asked her.

"At Walmart on Deans Bridge Road," she answered, then looked down at the floor of the ambulance and thought about how all this started in the first place. Nu Nu was the only thing that she could picture. She cursed Sean out silently. *Out here fucking with other bitches have almost cost me my life.* Then she got a hold of herself. "Look, I got to go. You got my all my information, call me or drop by if you need me." She stood up, touched the lady on her shoulder, and in a light tone of voice, she said to her, "Thank you for everything." She tried to address them both at the same time.

IT HAD BEEN A LONG NIGHT FOR ASIA. SHE WENT AROUND THE apartment looking for her iPhone. When she found it, she dialed her mother's number. It was one thirty-seven in the morning and she answered on the third ring.

"Hey." Was all her mother said from the other end.

"Mom, I had a small situation, and I was wondering if I could come stay with you for a few days."

Without any hesitation, her mother said. "Do I need to come and get you," her mother asked with alarmed concern.

That alone was relief within itself, causing Asia to shed tears and break down. "Yes ma'am, I do." She dropped her face in her hand, allowing the tears to flow uncontrollably.

* * *

SEAN WAS A YOUNG TWENTY-ONE-YEAR OLD THUG WITH A BIG CHIP on his shoulder and nothing to lose. He was sitting at a raggedy table in his auntie's kitchen sweating bullets. Sitting on the table in front of him was a black plastic ashtray filled with white cocaine; he dipped the tip of a straw down into it, filled it up, brought it up to his nose, and took a long deep sniff. "Umph, this shit raw," he said out loud and looked up at Freda, his auntie. She was sitting in the chair next to him at the table. "Where you get this from," he asked her.

Freda had a lit Newport dangling from her black lips; she was a chocolate skin tone female in her late forties. She tried her best to keep herself made up, a pretty decent wig or weave every now and then; however, she had a drug problem that had a major hold on her. Cocaine was her choice of drug, along with marijuana, alcohol, and she went through a pack of Newport cigarettes a day. Sean was her sister's son. She passed away in her sleep when Sean was twelve; after that, he was in and out of the juvenile system, staying with friends until they couldn't allow it anymore. By the time he turned fourteen, he was in the streets stealing cars, smoking marijuana, and selling drugs.

Freda pulled on her Newport, filled her lungs up and then blew out a straightline stream of smoke. "Them gang members over there across the street. Them lil' boys don't know what they got." Her eyes were wide and glossy. Then she asked him, "So, why did you shoot up that girl's house, Sean? She a cool lil chick."

Sean's eyes went to her, stared at her for a moment, then he shrugged his shoulders. "Tell you the truth, auntie... I don't even know why I did that stupid ass shit." He paused for a moment and took a deep breath. "But what I do know is that I'm about to leave Augusta."

"Tuh, you better," she told him, and pulled the ashtray in front of her. After she took a couple of snorts, she wrinkled up her nose and looked at him. "And dude, you need to start prayin'. You doing too much out here in these streets not to be prayin'." She stood up. About no more than two feet away from her was the refrigerator, she quickly opened the door and pulled out a Michelob beer. She went back to the table and looked at Sean; he was holding his phone in his hand and smiling. When she noticed that he hadn't thought about anything she said, she just sat back down, removing the top and turning up her beer.

Sean looked up from the phone and stood up. "Auntie, my ride just pulled up," he said. "I'm out." He walked over to her, leaned down and kissed her on her cheek.

"Sean, be careful out there in them streets," she said as he was heading out the back door.

"Safe or careful? Whatever come my way, I'm good." He looked at her just before he opened the door. "You said pray, right?" He smiled and closed the door. When he got outside, it was dark and early in the morning. He walked around to the front of the house and moved across the worn-down grass. Nu Nu was parked in the driveway in her Tundra pickup truck. He could smell the marijuana smoke as he approached the driver side door. When he climbed up inside and closed the door, she looked at him; she had a smirk on her face and she was high as a kite. She passed him the blunt. When he took it, she put the truck in reverse and slowly backed out the driveway. Then she looked at him. "Where you wanna go," she asked him.

Sean pulled on the blunt, looking out the window as they begin cruising down the street. He was thinking to himself for a moment, then he finally looked at her. "Let's go on the run like *Queen and Slim*."

Nu Nu laughed as she looked out the front window. "Nigga, you must be out yo' rabbit ass mind," she said. "Just smoke that blunt and rest your nerves."

Sean had to laugh at that himself, and then he leaned back in his seat a little. With his window rolled down, he allowed the wind to blow and carry the smoke out. He was thinking to himself, something he'd barely ever did. His mind went back to a few hours ago when he made that stupid move. *What was you thinking?* he finally asked himself and pulled on the blunt again. He closed his eyes and said in a low voice, "You the one got me in all this bullshit."

Nu Nu didn't respond; she just kept driving and looking straight ahead. She turned on Meadowbrook Drive. Still riding in pure silence, she finally cut her eyes over at him; he still had his eyes closed. She looked back at the road and continued to drive. She made another right and drove up a steep street that had small red brick houses on each side. Most of the front yards were unkept grass. She finally began to slow down when she got to the end of the street, which happens to be a dead end. Nu Nu made a right and turned up the driveway of a three-bedroom red brick house that was trimmed in yellow chipped paint. She pulled the truck all the way into the backyard and parked it nearly on the patio that was only a slab of concrete. Sean finally opened his eyes and noticed that he was in Nu Nu's backyard.

She parked the truck and switched off the engine, and then she looked at him. "Are you coming in or what?"

Sean looked at her. "Do I have a choice," he said in a cold dry tone and opened the door.

Nu Nu opened her door and stepped down from the truck. She closed the door and went in the house through the sliding glass door. Sean was nearly on her heels, examining her wide hips and booty that had a nice jiggle to it when she walked. His mind was all over the place. He walked in and slid the door closed behind him. Nu Nu turned on the lights in the den area where they were. Sean wasn't a stranger to her house. He stepped over the toys and the pile of clothes that was in the middle of the floor and headed down the carpeted hallway. Nu Nu's room was the last one on the right. He walked in and sat on the bed, removing his gun from his waist and easing it underneath the pillow. Then he removed his shoes and laid back on the bed.

Nu Nu walked in and closed the door behind her, locking it. She was wearing a pair of loose fitting shorts and a black halter top. She started taking off her clothes and then climbed in the bed and laid next to him. Without question, she knew that Sean was stressing and that he had a lot of stuff on his mind. She got up close to him; her nipples were erect, and her breasts were firm. Sean was laying on his back with his left arm underneath his head. Nu Nu breathed on his neck; he felt her warm breath and then the wetness from her tongue. He finally turned over and faced her. "I'on even know why I keep fuckin' with you," he said to her.

Nu Nu moved her hands down between his legs, carefully massaging his wood. He jumped a little and his stomach muscles tightened. She whispered, "Cause, you only love good pussy, a bitch that's gonna squirt all over that dick. And you know I'm the only bitch that will let you have your way. You said she wasn't pleasin' you, that she couldn't cook and was always working."

Sean listened at everything she said. *Damn! Maybe I told this bitch too much, now she using it against me.*

Nu Nu unzipped his pants and freed his wood. He was on soft, but he was thick and growing in her hand. At the same time, he eased his hands down between her legs, and as soon as he touched her vagina, she was instantly wet, and that was Sean's weakness right there. He moved his face closer to hers and put his lips on her earlobe. She tasted salty, he knew it was dried up sweat, but he didn't care. Nu Nu tensed up a little. Then she whispered, "You know that shit be drivin' me crazy."

Sean felt her body heating up, and her nipples were growing harder by the second. She carefully climbed on top of him, spreading her thighs on either side of his, then she reached underneath herself and clutched his thick wood. Nu Nu rotated her waist as she worked the head of his wood in between her wet vagina. "You gonna take it all tonight or are you gonna run from it," he said to her as he stared into her eyes.

Nu Nu wanted to take all of him, but Sean was working with a full package beef sausage that hooked with a deep curve and was decorated with thick veins. She eased down further on him, pressing her lips tight together as she went. He put his hands on her waist and gripped her tight, pulling her down on him and forcing his wood deep up inside her.

"Ohhhhh, shit!" she yelled out in pain.

"That's what I like to hear." He growled like a mad man, and for the next forty minutes, they had sex in every position that was possible. Sean was dripping sweat and so was Nu Nu. They were now laying in bed in the dark, sharing a Newport cigarette. Nu Nu was laying on her side with her head propped up with her hand. She was looking at Sean as he stared up at the ceiling.

"I'm 'bout to get up out of Augusta," he told her as he exhaled a stream of smoke from his mouth.

"Where are you gonna go," she asked him while drawing small circles on his shoulder with the tip of her fingernail.

Sean hesitated before he responded. He didn't have a clue in the world where he was going to go. He didn't have a car of his own, and he definitely didn't have enough money to get too far. He shifted his head toward Nu Nu. "How much money you got?"

"Eight hundred I got to give Rent-A-Center for this this furniture," she said truthfully. "But if you need it, you can get it."

"Okay, that will get me to Atlanta. I'm just gonna go up there and duck off until this shit blows over." He finally said with pure confidence in his voice, sitting all the way up in bed and swinging his legs over to the side. Sean sat there for a moment, slumped over at the waist with the cigarette still smoking from between his fingers. He pulled on it one more time and snubbed it out in the filthy ashtray that was sitting there on the nightstand. When he blew out the smoke, he flipped his head back and looked at Nu Nu.

"How the fuck can a nigga's luck be so bad that I shoot through the wall and hit the old lady next door?" It came from his mouth as a question, but he just wanted to vent about the situation. It was unreal to him, and it was bothering him, had his head messed up.

Nu Nu rubbed her hand across his back to comfort him with any kind of support that she could give. She moved up closer to him, his body was warm. "You just got to try to forget about it," she finally whispered.

Sean laughed with one hard 'ha ha' sound. He stood up, stepped in his jeans, and worked his feet inside his shoes. "It's not that easy, Nu Nu," he said to her. "Now let me get that money so I can get out of here."

CHAPTER 4

*a*sia hadn't stayed in her mother's place in nearly two years; she was young and strong and had a lot to prove when it came to her parents. She was sitting in a high chair in her mother's kitchen at the island. Her mother, Kim, was standing across from her in front of the stove, still dressed in her night clothes; nothing more than a long gray t-shirt with pink embossed letters that read: *We Are Angels* across the front and a pair of fuzzy slippers to match. Her skin was brown and smooth, and her hair was wrapped in a tie up flimsy rag. She dipped her spoon down in her bowl of cereal and carefully slipped it into her mouth, a few chews, and then she said to Asia, "Your dad is going to be pissed once he finds out about this."

Asia was looking down at her phone when her mother's words cut through the air, causing her to lift her head and stare at her. Asia was trusting her mother to keep her business away from her father. She didn't want that. Her dad was *extra*, as she called him. He turned the smallest thing into a big issue. "So, you're gonna tell him?" Asia asked her mother in a serious tone of voice.

Kim's eyebrows raised up a little as she looked at her daughter. She put her spoon in the bowl of cereal and placed the palms of her hands face down on the granite countertop. "I was hoping *you* would," she said to her.

Asia slowly shook her head from side to side; her eyes were still staring at her mother. She wasn't trying to break her stare because she wanted to let her know that she was very serious.

"I'm not. I have enough going on, and I definitely don't need his unkind words right now."

"Your so-called boyfriend *shot* at you and had every intention on hurting you, and you don't want your dad to know?"

Asia jumped up and slapped her hand on the granite top. "No, and I mean it," she yelled at her mother.

Kim pointed her finger. "Don't raise your voice at me, especially in my damn house," she warned. Her face was twisted up now and her forehead was wrinkled.

Asia stood there for a brief moment, thinking about everything that was going on in her life right now. Sean had her scared to death, and her dad had her just as scared. And now here she was, raising her voice at her own mother. She allowed her eyes to close for a brief moment, the room fell silent. Asia's eyes begin to tear, and she just looked down at the kitchen counter and stared at it. When she finally got herself and her thoughts together, she raised her head and looked at her mother.

Kim was staring at her face, still looking somewhat angry. "So, that's what hanging out in the hood and the streets do to you?"

"...maybe it do," Asia said and turned around, moving toward the stairs. As she was walking up them, she yelled back over her shoulder. "I'm out of your house as soon as I get my stuff."

"Fine, and when you leave this time, don't come back," Kim yelled back. Her eyes followed Asia as she went further up the stairs and faded away from her eyesight. "Sassy mouth bitch."

* * *

TWO HOURS LATER, ASIA WAS SITTING IN HER CAR IN THE PARKING lot of a cheap motel on Washington Road. She was parked only a couple of spaces away from the front entrance. From the driver seat, she sat and thought, *This shit is for the birds. I am not about to be living like this.* She couldn't do nothing but shake her head in pure disgust. She saw the Spanish cleaning lady coming out of the room that she'd checked in. Asia switched off her car, got out, grabbed her bag from the backseat, and walked across the parking lot, going straight to her room. Once she got inside and locked the door, the next thing she did was turned on the air conditioner and kicked off her shoes so she could relax for a moment. There was a queen-sized bed that looked comfortable and cozy. She sat down on it and faced the window; the curtain was closed, and the air conditioner unit was right beneath it. *I hope this clown isn't out here looking for me,* she thought, then she pulled out her iPhone and rolled over on her back. She was about to call her best friend, but the outgoing call was interrupted by an incoming Facetime call. Asia's eyebrows bunched together when she tried to figure out who was calling. She answered the call and Angelo's face appeared in the phone screen.

The first thing that he said was, "Well, hello." His smile was charming.

Asia was caught off guard, but she flashed him a smile back. "Hey, Angelo," she said back to him.

"Oh, you remembered my name," he hinted with a bigger smile.

"Of course, why would I forget," she said back. Her smile was wide and bright for the first time in a long time.

"Man, you wanna hear something that's crazy?" He asked her.

Asia really couldn't believe that he had anything crazier to say than what she had going on, but she said, "Sure, why not." Her shoulders shrugged as she said it.

"I'm still in Georgia," he told her. "Just in the next town over from you."

Asia gave a confused look now; her smile had faded a little. She was hoping that everything was alright with him. "What next town? I thought you'd be in Texas by now."

"Waynesboro, Georgia. We got pulled over in this lil hick town, and they confiscated my racecar, tryin' to say it's stolen. Which it's not. Anyway, I'll be here until later tonight. Maybe we can have dinner or something before I leave if you're free."

Asia was caught all the way off guard with that question; it was too soon to be seeing anyone else right now. Her mind wasn't working right. Or was it? She pressed her lips together and thought long and hard for a moment. Then she said to him, "Tell you the truth, I would love to. But I got so much drama going on in my life right now that I wouldn't be able to focus."

"Hey, life comes with drama, life comes with issues. It's nothin' more than your test that you'll have to past in order to give your testimony at some point."

"Yeah...But..."

"Listen, Asia. I'm about to come up there just to see you. My uncle is with me, but he's staying down here until all the paper-work is cleared on the car. Tell me a good location that we can meet at."

She took another deep breath.

He was smiling at her through the phone.

"I'm in a shitty motel room right now. The Red Roof Inn on Washington Road."

She watched him pick up another phone and type in the location; he looked back up at her and said. "Destination time says forty-three minutes. I'll call you when I get in the parking lot." And before she could say another word, he ended the call.

Asia looked at her phone, stared at it for a brief moment.

"Dang, you could've at least waited to let me say yes or no," she said in a low tone of voice. Then she laid there for another five minutes before she got up and went and took a shower.

* * *

JUST A LITTLE UNDER AN HOUR, ANGELO WAS PULLING INTO THE parking lot of the Red Roof Inn motel; he was driving a rental car that he'd brought from Texas. When he found a parking space and parked, he picked up his iPhone and dialed Asia's number, she answered on the second ring.

"Hello," she said.

"I'm outside. Are you ready?" he asked her.

"Yes. I'm coming out now."

Angelo was nearly parked in front of her room, so he saw her walk out of one of the doors on the first floor, and he still had her on the phone. "I see you; I'm right here parked. Stay there and I'm coming to you." Then he hung up the phone. He pulled out of the space and backed nearly in a U-shape until he was right in front of her.

Where Asia was standing, all she had to do was open the car door. She did, and then she got in and closed the door, looking at him with a smile. The first thing that she noticed was the wonderful smelling cologne that had her in a daze. She strapped in her seatbelt and said, "Hey."

Angelo pulled the car in drive; his foot was still on the brake. "Miss shy lady," he said with a smile and that pure southern tone of voice did something to her.

"I'm not shy," she said back to him.

Angelo slowly eased out of the parking lot and headed onto Washington Road. It was a little after noon and the traffic wasn't bumper to bumper, but it was busy. "Have you had lunch?" he asked her.

Asia flashed an elegant smile at him and shook her head, whispering in a low voice, "No."

"Sounds like a lunch date then. I found this cool little spot called Takosushi just around the corner from here. From the reviews, they have great sushi. Have you ever been there?"

"Takosushi?" she said, as if she was asking the question to herself. When she realized that she'd never heard of it before, she said. "I never been there before."

"Great, let me turn you on to something different. And how I'm new in your city and know more about it than you do?" He cocked his head sideways and flashed that smile again.

Asia's shoulders shrugged a little. "Honestly, I don't really do anything here. I work at Walmart and then I'm back home, just be low key staying to myself. But apparently that don't work."

Angelo was driving and checking the rearview mirror at the same time. He switched lanes and flipped on his right turn signal. He then cut his eyes over at her. "Sounds like some stress going on."

"What? You just don't understand," she said.

"Oh, trust me, I understand. I know how that goes. Especially if it's concerning the baby mamas and the baby daddies."

Asia laughed. "Right." Was all she said, and then she got quiet for a moment. They continued to ride in silence for few more minutes. Angelo turned on the radio and adjusted his music to a song called Love Calls by the artist Kem. And just then, Asia looked at him, her entire demeanor changed. "I love that song," she said, and began moving her neck and body, singing along with Kem.

He gave her a smile. "One of my favorites as well," he said as they were pulling up into the Surry Center parking lot. The restaurant was just to their left, and Angelo parked nearly in front of the door. There were four iron tables lined up outside with green umbrellas covering each one.

"Look like a pretty chill spot," he said. Then he asked her, "You want to eat outside?"

Asia thought about Sean, and she thought about the girl Nu Nu that was stalking her; she would love to eat outside, but she was paranoid and would hate for anybody to see her and it brought more problems than what she already had. "We can eat on the inside," she finally said. She looked around in the parking lot, realizing that she'd never been on that side of town. She finally opened the car door, and as she was stepping out, Angelo was stepping out from the driver side. They both closed their doors at the same time.

Angelo walked around toward the front of the car, and Asia headed in the same direction. He carefully placed his right hand in the center of her back so she could walk in first. As they approached the front door, a petite blond greeted them both and escorted them to a table in the corner just by the window. The restaurant itself wasn't that crowded; there was a couple sitting at the bar and two females were sitting at a table on the other side. Asia sat down on the cushion side of the table and Angelo took the chair. The menus were placed in front of them. Angelo looked over at Asia. "Why you look worried? Like something is on your mind."

Asia moved her eyes up and looked at him. "Do I really," she asked him, trying her best to keep her composure. She picked up her phone from the table and turned on the camera, looking at herself in the reflection. "I don't look worried," she lied out loud.

"If I can help you, I will. If you don't relax and let me know what's the business, there's nothing that I can do."

Asia sat in total silence for a moment, placing her phone back down on the table. Just as she was about to say something, a waiter appeared at the table, carrying two glasses of water. Sitting one in front of each of them, Angelo looked up at him.

"Bring me two of your best sushi rolls and a glass of red wine for me," he told him.

The waiter looked at Asia. "And you, Ma'am?"

Asia looked down at the menu, she didn't know what to order, and then she noticed that they had burgers. She looked up at him. "Just the burger and fries. I'll also have a glass of wine I guess."

"Great, I'll get everything out to you in a few minutes," he said, and walked off towards the back.

Angelo watched him as he left, then his eyes went back to Asia. "Back to where we were," he said as he slid his elbows upon the table and propped his head on top of his hands.

"I guess when I think about this mess, it doesn't seem real, not real in my life anyway." She paused and took a long deep breath. For the next hour, she explained everything to Angelo, word for word on how her life had went from sugar to dumpster juice in the last forty-eight hours. They talked and sipped wine. They laughed together and ate, then they talked some more. Asia learned a lot about the Texas stranger, and she was interested in learning more.

Angelo was on his third glass of red wine; apparently, it wasn't affecting him because he was still looking the same and his voice wasn't dragging. He took another sip, sat his glass down, and said to her, "Honestly, I think you need a vacation away from Augusta." His eyes were dead on her, but before she could respond, his iPhone began to buzz. He paused and picked it up right after holding up one finger, telling her to hold on for a second while he took the call. He saw that it was his uncle calling; he answered, and they chatted for a minute.

Then two minutes passed.

Three minutes went by.

Now a little after five minutes, he nodded his head with a smile and finally hung up the phone and smiled at Asia. "I got my end situated, we got the car, we got that flatbed, and it's a go," he said.

"That's great," Asia responded back with a smile.

Angelo's face turned serious and still; he folded his arms across his chest. "Now for you, the first thing you're going to do is get out that cheap ass motel." Then he picked up his phone and did a quick search and found a better hotel, dialing the number from the website. Soon as he dialed it, a soft tone voice woman answered from the other end.

"Hello, I want to book a room, king size bed, for a week."

"And when will you be checking in," The lady asked from the other end.

Angelo looked at Asia; she had a confused look on her face. He spoke back into the phone. "Today for sure." He nodded his head at Asia.

She smiled and nodded her head back at him. For the next few minutes, Angelo gave the lady his information, and when he hung up with her and sat his phone down on the table, he reached across the table and put his finger underneath her chin. "After your week is up, and when you check out, I'll have you a spot set up in Dallas. Will you come?"

Asia froze for a moment. That question came so fast she didn't know what to say, so she swallowed. Her eyes were still on his. "I..."

"Look." He cut her off and said, "You don't have to make that decision right now. I'm sorry about that. What about you come visit first, check it out? And if you don't like it, I'll keep trying until you do." He laughed and flashed a bright smile that lit up the room.

"Okay," was all Asia said. Her eyes were boring straight into his; she wanted to ask more questions, but at this point, she was like, *What the hell. I need a break.*

CHAPTER 5

The following morning, Asia awoke in a huge king-sized bed at the Marriott Hotel. The room was dark and comfortable, feeling like she was in the clouds. Underneath the thick blanket and in between the cool sheets, she stretched her arms and flexed her shoulders all at the same time. Her yawn sounded more like a moan. When she finally got up, the first thing she did was take her phone from the nightstand and looked at. She had a text message from Imani. When she opened it and read it, her eyes stretched wide. It was a mugshot photo of Sean from the local Augusta newspaper. The caption read: **This dude is STUPID STUPID. They got him, but dude shot at the police trying to get away.**

Asia's eyes stretched wide in disbelief; she seriously couldn't believe what she was reading and hearing. She went to Google and pulled up the link to read for herself. For the next few minutes, she moved her lips and read the article in silence, checking to see if it said anything about her. And just what she was afraid of, there her name was, jumping out at her, and she nearly screamed. Asia shook her head from side to side in disgust; after she closed it, she couldn't do anything else but sit in silence for a few minutes. Then she dialed Imani's number, and she answered it on the third call.

"Giiirrrllll," her voice sung out from the other end. "Did you see that shit?"

"I'm at a lost for words right now," Asia said. She swallowed and continued to talk. "This shit is so messed up, and they got my name all in it. My dad is gonna trip the fuck out for real."

"Oh, you haven't told him yet?" Imani asked.

"Nah, my Mom know. And I'm sure she's going to let him know."

"Damn!" Imani shot back. "What are you gonna do?"

Asia got quiet, her eyes went to the wall, and then down to the floor. When she spoke back into the phone, she said in a simple tone of voice. "I'm going to Texas for a little while. I'm not trying to go to court or nothing."

"So, you're going down there with ole boy that you met?" she asked from the other end.

"I was already thinking about it, but since this happened, I'm really going now. I mean, ain't nothing else here for me, Imani."

"Friend, you got to do you. You don't have any kids, you young, and you smart. Shit, go for it."

Asia's eyes lit up and she smiled, then she got sad again. "Been hurt, lied to. Used and broken all by the same nigga. I got to leave."

"I feel you on that, friend," Imani said with a sound of emotion in her voice; she was feeling every ounce of pain that Asia was going through. And for any woman, it hurt like hell. But that's where the toughness of a woman comes in. Asia drifted into a long deep thought for a moment. Her life was playing in her mind. Her childhood days as a little girl, watching the Cosby show where she envisioned herself as Rudy and her life would be just as it was on TV. But now she'd grown up and realized that it wasn't anywhere near that. She shook her head as her eyes began to tear up and turn moist. She said, "I'm coming to see you before I leave."

"Great, just call me and let me know when you're coming."

"I can come now, I'm leaving tomorrow. The longer I stay, the more depressed I get."

"Friend, you probably don't need to come now," Imani said from the other end. "I got a little extra shit going on right now."

"Okay, I understand," Asia said, sounding a little disappointed, but she didn't allow it to get in her way. "I'll call you with an update." She hung up the phone, looked at it, and tossed it on the bed. Asia tried her best to pull herself together, but it seemed as if something was tugging at her heart. When she leaned down and picked up her phone, she looked at it and pulled up her dad's contact and called his number. As the sound of the phone rang in her ear, there were a million and one things going through her mind. After the fourth ring, she heard his voice come through with a deep drawl, as if she'd just woke him up from a deep sleep.

"I already heard the bad news. This call has to be great news."

Asia twisted her mouth in one corner and rolled her eyes at the same time. For the next ten seconds, there was a wave of silence between the both of them. She finally said. "I just want to apologize to you, Dad."

"Apologize to me for what," he responded back kind of quick. Then his next words hit her like a brick. "I'm **done** with you, Asia. The whole situation. You like to run around in the streets and bust your legs open for nothing ass niggas. Why stop now?"

At that moment, Asia felt as if her heart had stopped. She was motionless and looking down at the floor as her tears began to flow. Then without warning...

CLICK!

He'd hung up. Asia couldn't believe it. She sat there for the next thirty minutes crying her eyes out. She knew her dad was strict and true to his word, but she didn't expect him to flip on her like that. She finally got up and walked into the bathroom and looked at herself in the mirror, like the mirror was going to talk back to her, even though the mirror couldn't talk. Asia just felt that the reflection of herself was the only person that she had to talk to. She hated to see herself crying and all in an emotional state of mind. "Fix yourself up," she said to her reflection and moved her hands to the top of her head as if she was really wearing a crown; she moved her hand as if she was adjusting it. "There," she said, and then wiped the tears from her face with the back of her hand. Asia turned on the cold water in the sink and allowed it to run for a moment. She cupped her tiny hands underneath the running water, slightly bent over the sink, and splashed the water in her face. Then she stood up and looked at herself again, giving herself a smile and putting her hands on her hips as if she was posing. Asia had a nice figure, her body was shaped and curvy, and her face was beautiful. She knew it, and she knew she was worth more than what Sean had to offer. She finally moved away from the mirror and turned on the shower. After taking off all her clothes, she went back into the bedroom and grabbed her iPhone. She pulled up Angelo's name and sent him a text: **I'm ready to come**. She sent it and stared at the phone until it said it was delivered. She waited for a moment. After she didn't get a response, she went into the bathroom, and stepped inside the shower, and took her phone with her. She sat it on the ledge away from the water. She began lathering up her washcloth and slowly washing every crevice of her body. She watched how the water and suds rolled down her round firm breasts, her nipples were a rose-pink color. She took that complexion from her mother. And she definitely loved it. Asia turned around, allowing the warm water to massage her neck and back. She closed her eyes in hopes of escaping reality. And that's when she heard her phone. She turned around and saw that it was Angelo calling her through Facetime. "Shit." She said in a low tone as she answered it. But she brought the phone up, so he could only see her face. He flashed his handsome smile at her.

"Good morning," he said.

His voice lit up her insides and brought a bright smile on the corner of her lips. "Hello, Angelo. You get my message?"

"Yes, I did. And it made my day," he said. "But I have one problem, nothing major. I'll be in Vegas for the next couple of days on a business trip, you're more than welcome to come and then we'll head back to Texas after that."

"Ummm, I never been to Vegas," she said.

"What?" Angelo nearly shouted with a serious and playful look all at the same time. "Listen, you got to come out here with me. You'll never want to leave. Lots of fun. It'll be like your mini vacation."

Asia was taking it all in and smiling ear to ear at the same time. She looked at him, square in his eyes. "I'm coming, but I don't have any of my things packed at the apartment or nothing."

Angelo thought for a second, and then he said. "Just get all your personal things, you don't need any furniture or clothes. Just get it, then call me. I'll fly you straight out there, okay."

"Okay," she finally said.

"And I just got to say this. You have a very elegant smile."

"Thank you."

"And beautiful breasts," he said and hung up the phone just before blowing her a kiss. Asia gave a crushing smile as if she just met her boyfriend after a high school football game. When she finally stepped out the shower, she felt full of life again. Maybe *bliss* was the word that described her at that moment.

She was now about to start her new journey, and only God knows where it was about to take her.

BOOK 2
LAS VEGAS

CHAPTER 6

*A*ngelo was a natural boss. When you hear the phrase, "Get it out the mud," they should have his face trending all across the Internet underneath the caption. He grew up in Houston, Texas, in a crime area called Sunnyside. Day in and day out, there was always something going on. Drug dealing, arm robberies, murder, pimping. You name it, he'd seen it all. But Angelo was smart and sharper than your typical dope boy or local hustler. And that was mainly because he came from a family of hustlers, but most of the time, the family either become a victim to their own supply, wind up with a heavy prison sentence, or earn a beautiful headstone, some flowers, and several RIP's on your social media pages. Angelo was a tad bit smarter than the rest of the family. He did his dirt in the streets, but he graduated from a small community college and earned his associate degree in business. He owned several rental properties in Texas, earning money from Airbnb, and he had his own tow trucking company. He owned racecars and hair salons and loved to gamble at the roulette table. But the one thing that Angelo didn't have was a woman, and it wasn't because he couldn't get one. He simply was always on the go and trying to get money and handle his business. Now, don't get it wrong, Angelo was indeed a major boss in his city, and his name carried a lot of weight when it came to women.

But that was another story.

It was *him* that was parked out front at the airport in Vegas waiting for Asia, not a driver, not a friend, not an Uber, nor a cab. But it was him, and he was behind the wheel of a black 2020 Range Rover with dark tinted windows and high rims. He had Asia on the phone, guiding her straight to him. When he saw her, he stepped out and walked around the front of the Range, smiling as he hugged her. She was carrying a small bag. He took it from her shoulder and opened her door for her. "We don't have far to drive; we're staying at the MGM," he said to her.

Asia looked at him, staring him in his eyes. He was staring back, caught up in her beauty. And at the same time, he was hoping that she wasn't just another woman that was after his money and wanted to look good on his shoulder. He grinned at her. "Why you lookin' like that?" he asked her with a smile.

She shrugged lightly. "I'm just glad to be here with you I guess," she said back to him. Then she hugged him, and he hugged her back. His cologne was seeping up in her nose, her face was in his chest, and then she whispered, "My God, you smell so good."

He pulled back from her, leaned down, and kissed her on her cheek. "Thank you. Now we got to move. I got some people waiting for us."

When they got in the Range Rover, Asia was taken by surprise at how comfortable and clean it felt on the inside. Her mind was flipping and turning in so many different directions. Angelo was different than any other man that she'd ever met in her whole entire life. She felt a feeling that she hadn't ever felt before. As they rode, she was taking in the bright sunshine, and her eyes were filled with excitement.

"How's was your flight," he asked her, breaking the silence.

Asia turned toward him. "Honestly, from Augusta to Atlanta, it wasn't too good. But from Atlanta to here, it was great. I just watched *Black Panther* on the way here and took a nap. That was it."

"*Black Panther?*" he said. Then he looked back at the street.

"Yes, you never seen it?" she asked him.

"I wanted to. But by the time I decided to go see it, everyone had told me what it was about. So, I took it off my list."

"Oh no. I have to take you to see it. Trust me, you'll love it."

Angelo nodded as he turned into the MGM Grand. He said to her, "We can do that, but you never know. You just might meet the star of the movie out here. It's always some type of event going on out here."

Asia didn't respond with her mouth, only just a slight nod of her head; she wasn't about to set herself up for anything that would come back and bite her in the future. They'd finally pulled up to the front of the casino, and a slim handsome guy walked up to the driver side of the Range as Angelo was putting the SUV in park. He opened the door and Angelo stepped out and left it running. He tipped the valet and walked around to the passenger side and opened the door for Asia. When she stepped down, she couldn't help herself as she looked around at all the expensive cars, the Rolls Royces, Bentleys, Lambos, you name it, they were coming through. The engines on some of the sports cars were roaring and echoed off the buildings. She turned around, walking in stride with Angelo. Just before they entered the glass doors to the lobby, a petite blond female pulled up to the curb in a canary yellow Lamborghini. The driver door rose up, and she stepped out in a Raiders jersey; and if she had on anything else besides her high heel Red Bottoms, you couldn't tell. Without a word, she hurried inside and left the door up and the car running.

Angelo said to Asia as they were walking inside, "If I told you that she was a prostitute, would you believe me?"

"No, I wouldn't," she responded.

"And that's why I wouldn't tell you." He laughed. They entered the fancy lobby and walked through the crowded area. Angelo led Asia straight to the elevators, allowing her to walk inside first, then he walked right behind her. There was another couple that entered with them as well. Angelo pressed the button for the thirty-second floor and then moved behind Asia, placing his hands upon her shoulders. Asia relaxed up against him. He massaged her shoulders as they rode to the elevator music. It rose up to the thirteenth floor and came to a stop. The door opened and the couple got off and the doors closed again. "Are you hungry?" he asked her.

"I'm not sure," she responded back.

Angelo moved his face in front of hers and in a playful manner, he said. "Either you hungry or you not. Don't start that too cute to eat mess." Then he placed his lips on hers without any warning whatsoever.

That took Asia by surprise, she wasn't ready for that at all. But she definitely didn't resist. She tilted her head back and felt his tongue move into her mouth. She closed her eyes and quickly got caught up in the moment. When the bell sounded, the doors parted and Angelo pulled away from her, grabbed her by her hand, and they walked out onto the floor that he had the room on. Without a word, they walked to the room. Angelo held up the card key to the door lock until it turned green. He entered and held the door for her to come in. "Make yourself at home," he said as he was closing the door and locking it.

Asia went in. She sat her bag down on the foot of the king-sized bed, then she walked over to the floor to ceiling window and stared down at the breathtaking scenery below. "This is beautiful," she said as Angelo moved up behind her. He wrapped his arms around her waist and pressed his face up against hers.

They stared out the window together. The cars were tiny down below and the sun was bright as could be.

"Vegas is kind of like my getaway spot from Texas," he said in a low tone. "So, if you decide to move to Texas with me, just know I'm out here every other week, you're welcome to come if you want."

"I just want to get myself situated first," she said and curled herself up in his arms.

"Situated as in what?"

"Like a job."

"You already hired," he said.

"Oh yeah, what's my position?"

He smiled. *Face down.* He allowed the joke to play in his head.

"Just be yourself, be real. And look pretty while you're doing it." He smiled at her and his tone of voice was insurance enough to make her believe him.

Asia felt his powerful arms squeeze her body, that alone made her relax and feel secure. Her question to his last statement would have to go on hold. However, she let out a light whisper, "I can do that." Then she turned around and faced him. Angelo had a different aura around him; as she stared into his eyes, he stared back into hers. And for the next sixty-three seconds, they just held one another. No kissing. No touching, just smiling and staring at one another. Then she whispered. "I wanna take a shower." Her hands moved into his palms.

"Sounds good," he said. "I need to make a few calls while you're doing that. And when you finish, we going shopping and out to eat."

"Sounds great to me," Asia said and headed toward the bathroom, grabbing her bag on her way there. Angelo watched her as she walked off, her hips swaying in a rhythm like slow moving water. He had to smile; her body was nice and young, firm and curvy.

When the door finally closed in the bathroom, he pulled his

iPhone from his pocket and went to the Internet. He sat down in the chair on the other side of the room and pulled up the sports betting site. He was a big gambler and was good at what he did. It took him a few minutes to check the stats and the point spread, who was playing who and then he entered a two-pick on one ticket.

He entered a three-pick on another one. On another ticket, he took a head up bet with a nice payout if he hit. After that, he got up, and he removed his shoes, leaving them there in the middle of the floor. He went over to the bed, sat down on the foot of it. Angelo removed his shirt. His upper body was sculpted with elegance. His structure was similar of a corner back that was still in the NFL. Angelo was tired, he'd been up all night on the gambling tables downstairs. He leaned back and laid down, and in the next few minutes, he was in a deep sleep, with his left arm folded underneath his head. For the next few minutes, he slept in peace, his chest rising up and down and his lips slightly parted.

Asia finally walked into the bedroom. She was wrapped in a towel with nothing on underneath. She actually had preplanned her intro. But when she saw that Angelo was knocked out and in a deep sleep, she didn't attempt to bother him. Instead, she just climbed in the bed next to him, moving easy and carefully so as not to disturb him.

Now Angelo was a light sleeper, so he felt her as soon as she got into the bed. He stirred, looked over at her. She paused, they looked at each other.

"I tried my best not to wake you," she said.

He reached and grabbed her, pulled her to him. "You can't creep too good I see." That was the last thing he said to her before he kissed her and began working the towel away from her body. Asia laid on top of his chest, and Angelo allowed his strong hands to move down her back slowly until he touched her curves and firm round butt.

"Do you have any condoms?" she asked him in a low whisper, nibbling on his earlobe.

"Yes," he said back to her, then pulled her body up until she was straddling his face. Angelo's heartbeat sped up a few notches, and so did hers. The opening of her shaved vagina was nearly at his top lip. Then he brushed his tongue across her clit and her entire body shook lightly. He felt it, gripped her ass cheeks, and pulled her down until he could massage her pussy lips with his own lips.

Asia began rotating her hips just enough to let him know that she wanted whatever he had to offer. She looked down at him, her hands were on the headboard for support. His mouth was soft and wet, and he had her pussy dripping like a faucet. Angelo tugged on her clitoris tongue with his lips, and then he allowed his tongue to work around it. Asia's legs trembled, only this time they didn't stop. She couldn't control herself; she was about to explode, and she was trying to pull back before she came like a gush of water; she didn't want to release it all over his face like that. But Angelo wanted whatever she had to give as well. His grip on her ass and waist tighten to the point that she had no choice but to allow her sweet juices to explode all in his mouth.

"That's right, baby," he said as he continued to suck on her as if her juices gave him some type of extra strength like Thanos had just received the last and final stone.

Asia wanted to pull away, it felt as if he knew exactly where every one of her nerves were, and that was driving her bat crazy. "It...God, it's good," she stuttered over her words.

"Come for me again," he said to her.

"Can I ride it? I need to feel it, pleaseeee," she begged.

Angelo ignored her. Tossing her to the side, he flipped her over on her stomach. "Lay there, don't move," he told her in a demanding tone, then he backed out of the bed and walked around to where the nightstand was at. He opened the drawer;

Asia's face was turned to the side where she could see him. His dick print was bulging through his jeans and she was impressed.

She couldn't help herself, she reached out and touched it. It was extremely hard. "I want it," she said, and began inching over toward the side where he was standing. Angelo pulled out a box of condoms and removed one from the box as she was unzipping his pants. By the time she freed his dick from the pee hole, she stuffed the head of it in her mouth first.

Angelo was impressed; she knew what she was doing, and she was nasty with it. Asia licked him from the bottom to the top and covered all nine inches with saliva. He placed his hand on the back of her head, and then she looked up at him. "Is it good to you?" she asked him, her eyes had a trance-like look in them.

Angelo pulled away from her and removed his pants and boxer briefs, all in one swift motion. He stepped out of them one foot at a time, and then he tore the condom open and rolled it on. He climbed onto the bed and pushed himself towards the middle.

Asia was looking at him, nearly stalking him at this point. When he finally got settled, she knew it was time for her to mount him. Inch by inch, she worked her body up on him and positioned her pink split just at the head of his dick. Slowly and carefully, she lowered her body down on him, feeling herself spreading faster than she thought.

"You driving the car, baby," Angelo said, and folded his arms behind his head. "I'm gonna try not to move."

"No, I want you to move. I want everything you have to offer." She closed her eyes and took a deep breath. And with that being said, she dropped all the way down on him until she felt it deep inside of her.

· · ·

Two hours later, Angelo was waking up again because his arm was cramping up where Asia was laying on it. She was curled up in his arms, her body pressed next to his as if they were one. He moved his arm from underneath her, and she rolled over and faced him. "When the sex put you to sleep, we don't have to question each other," he said and placed his lips on hers. They kissed, despite the sleeping breath.

"I don't even know what to say, Angelo…"

"Say you *my girl*, so we can start expanding this empire." He cut her off and rubbed the side of her face, his fingers tracing her face as if he was drawing on her skin.

"I'm your girl," she said with a smile. She whispered, "I'm ready for this new beginning."

"That's all I need to hear," he told her, and rolled on top of her. He didn't have to ask her to open her legs, she spread them open for him. Angelo was on his knees; he had his growing wood in his hand, and he moved it up and down against her wet pussy lips. "You want it," he asked her as he stared down into her eyes.

Asia didn't even answer, she reached and grabbed him and began stuffing it inside her. "Siiiiissss." She let out a hissing sound. Angelo pushed her legs back so far that her feet were nearly at her head. He looked down at her as he moved and worked his wood down inside of her. "I'm not sure if I'd be able to stay out of here," he said.

"It's all yours baby, you can stay in for as long as you want." Her words were so soft and seductive, and when she squirted all over him, he nearly lost his mind.

"Damn!" he said in pure amazement. And at that moment, Angelo knew he'd found something and someone special.

After they showered, Angelo took Asia right downstairs to one of the clothing stores and took her shopping for a few pieces of clothes. After that, they went over to the Wynn Hotel and Casino and shopped at a few more high-end stores like Louis Vuitton, Saint Laurent, and a few more other places. After her shopping spree, Asia had so much stuff that Angelo had to have it delivered to the hotel. They walked the Vegas strip, and Angelo took Asia on the boat ride while the guy sung to them as they cruised the small body of water. It was amazing how Vegas had so many attractions that a lot of people didn't know about.

The night turned into morning, and Asia and Angelo were having the time of their lives. For her, this was an experience that she had never had before. And of course, it seemed as if everything was moving so fast for her at this point. But that was life. And in real life, it can come fast or it can come slow. As for now, she was in her moment and she wasn't about to be denied. All she wanted was a good man at this point.

Angelo had already started to develop some type of feelings for Asia. From what he learned so far, she was a down to earth woman. After several conversations with her, he learned more and more every day. And with that alone, he felt as if that was beneficial for him as well. There weren't too many women that a man would meet and the woman would open up and be totally honest the first go round.

Angelo was sitting out on the hotel balcony in a recliner chair, just relaxing and staring out into the crisp blue morning sky. Asia was on the recliner with him, her back pressed against his chest. Maybe they were staring at the same sky.

Maybe they were thinking the same thing.

"You wanna hear somethin' funny?" he asked her. He had his arms draped around her shoulders. Asia moved a little, then she tilted her head back a little to let him know she was ready.

"I'd love to," she responded back in a soft voice.

Angelo took a deep breath, then another one. "I remember the first night I saw you sitting in Popeye's. I rehearsed three different approach lines that I wanted to say to you. And by the time I got to where you were sitting, I'd forgot every damn thing that I thought I was gonna say."

Asia turned around a little bit more, with a smile on her face. "Well, I'm so glad that you came over because when I first saw you, I was so nervous. I didn't know what to say or nothing. I actually had my best friend on the phone, and I even had to hang up with her." She let out a sigh of relief.

Angelo was staring in her eyes, and she was staring back in his. It was like a trance or shock was going on between the both of them. Then he said to her, "I'm interested to see where this can go. Of course, you know that we *go together* now."

She smiled, and then let out a small laugh. "Go together as in girlfriend and boyfriend, like in high school?"

Angelo burst out with laughter himself, and for the rest of the day they laughed, talked, and shared more of each other's history. However, Angelo still had a few things that he hadn't told Asia. But she was soon to find out.

CHAPTER 7

*L*ATER THAT NIGHT, they arrived at George Bush Intercontinental Airport in Houston, Texas. Angelo had a lot of business to take care of, but he wanted to make sure that Asia was comfortable with her surroundings first. After they got their luggage, Angelo already had a ride waiting for them as they exited the airport. It was a simple black SUV with tinted windows. As they began walking up toward it, there was a heavyset guy in a jogging suit and tennis shoes waiting for them at the rear. He extended his hand out to Angelo.

"Always good to see you back home from a safe business trip." He gave Angelo a hug and patted his back.

"And it's always good to see you holding everything in tack," he responded, and then he introduced him to Asia. "This is Asia," he said proudly.

The big guy put out a large fleshy hand in front of her. "Hello, Asia. It's always a pleasure to meet a queen. I'm Big Moe." He sounded like a grizzly bear.

Asia gave a smile and shook his hand. "Okay, Big Moe, it's a pleasure to meet you as well."

Moments later, Big Moe had all the bags neatly packed in the rear of the SUV. Asia and Angelo got in the backseat, and Big Moe got behind the wheel. As they drove, Angelo was on his iPhone sending out messages back to back. Big Moe looked in the rearview mirror at him. "First stop is?" he asked Angelo.

"The Ivy River Oaks," was all he said, and then he went back to his phone.

Asia was sitting next to him in pure silence. She was looking out the window, taking in the scenery. Houston was indeed a large city, and it seemed to be spread out across a lot of land. For the next few minutes, the only sound that could be heard was the tires rolling against the asphalt. Asia's phone rung, and it was the first time it did in two days. She pulled it from her pocket, looked at the screen, and saw a number that she didn't recognize at all. Should she answer? No. She didn't have a reason to at this point in her life. She was starting all the way over and had decided to leave the past in the past.

Angelo finally looked at her, reached over and grabbed her hand, wedging his fingers between hers. "You alright?" he asked her in a soothing tone.

She looked over at him, nodded her head, and said, "Yes," at the same time.

"Good, where we're heading to now is like a high-rise apartment. It's nice, I'm telling you."

"Is it your place," she asked him.

"I think so," he answered in a joking manner and pulled her hand up to his face and kissed it. "Of course, it's mines."

Asia didn't respond, she was feeling homesick already. She leaned over and placed her head on his shoulder and closed her eyes. She was thinking about her mother and father for some apparent reason. She didn't know if this was a good thing she was doing or a bad one. *What in the world am I doing,* she questioned herself, and then she felt her emotions getting all out of place.

When she wiped her teary eyes with the back of her hand,

Angelo looked down at her and noticed that she was crying. He swiftly placed his arms around her and held her tight. "What's wrong," he asked her in the softest voice that he could bring out.

Asia shrugged her shoulders slightly. "Just miss my parents. I feel like we ended on such a bad note."

Angelo didn't respond too fast; he wanted Asia to be comfortable, and even more, relaxed. And when he did respond, it was overwhelming. "I tell you what. If it'll make you feel better, if you would like me to fly back to Georgia with you to meet your parents and so you could tie up your loose ends, we can do that."

Asia took in his words. "Are you for real, Angelo?" she asked.

Angelo's face squenched up a little. "Am I for real? Why wouldn't I be?" he said to her, then added, "I want them to know you're safe and in good hands."

She sat in silence; her mind was wandering again. She was so emotional, thinking of what could go right and what could go wrong. Especially with her father. She knew he was a piece of work and very difficult at times. Besides that, she loved him. Asia slowly wrapped her arms around herself, then leaned in and kissed Angelo on his cheek. "Thank you," was all she said.

WHEN THEY ARRIVED AT THE IVY RIVER OAKS APARTMENTS, ASIA looked stunned at the high-rise building. The property came equipped with valet services, concierge services, and more. Big Moe dropped Angelo and Asia off in the front, and they walked through the lobby and took the elevator up to the ninth floor. Angelo was holding Asia's hand as they headed to the apartment door. He looked down at her. "I have one question for you," he said to her.

Asia looked up at him. "Okay, what is it?"

"Can you cook?"

Dude, you would ask me this when I got to pee, she thought, and said, "Well, yes. But not the fancy stuff in the restaurants."

They finally got to his door. Angelo inserted his key, turned the knob, and slowly pushed the door open. He extended his arm and allowed Asia to walk in first. When she stepped across the threshold of the studio apartment, she turned and faced him. She pressed her legs together and started moving side to side. "Where is the bathroom," she asked him in a near panic.

Angelo pointed. "First door on the right." Before he could turn around and close the door, Asia had spun around on her heels and nearly ran to the bathroom. When he heard the door close, he said out loud, "Alexa, turn on the lights."

The lights came on. He moved over toward the window, the curtains were already drawn. Angelo loved the view. That was one of the reasons why he got that apartment in the first place. He stood there for a minute until he heard the toilet flush. He turned around, went over to the cream-colored leather couch, and sat down for a moment. Asia came out and walked over to him. Asia stood in front of him, and he pulled her hand. "I would love to give you a tour tonight, but I'm tired as hell," he said.

Asia looked down at him, her eyes were low. She said, "I'm tired also." She placed her hands on his face, then Angelo pulled her down and positioned her so she could sit on his thigh. She leaned up against him, a long slow deep breath came from her. "Why do all this seem like a dream?" she asked him.

Angelo shrugged. "Asia." His voice was deep, clear, and sincere. "I'm not sure, but you'll have to think back and ask yourself if you deserve what you're receiving right now."

Asia thought long and hard about what he was saying. She nodded her head up and down, but she was looking out into nowhere fast. When she finally looked at him, she said. "Damn right I deserve it. This is what I've been asking for."

Angelo agreed with her, he smiled and nodded at the same

time. "Your opinion is what's important, baby. At any given moment, you can meet a nigga that'll promise you the world just to fuck. But when you know, you'll know. That's why it's never a rush with me because I don't want you to think I'm like these other clowns." He leaned in and kissed her softly.

She kissed him back. They shared a long hug, and he said to her, "Stand up." She stood up and he stood up as well. At that moment she was looking up at him, her eyes were slightly damp from his words that had took her by storm. He began rubbing her arms up and down, then moved his fingers along the spine of her back. He drew her close to him. He whispered, "Let go and let a real nigga love you and take care of you."

She stared in his eyes. A tear fell down her cheek. She smiled and said, "Okay, I'll give it a try. Just promise me one thing."

"I'm listening," he said.

"Please don't hurt me."

Angelo flashed a smile and nearly laughed out loud. "The only way that I'll hurt you is if you say, *it's too deep up in me.*"

Asia gave an embarrassing smile and playfully punched him in the chest. "Are you serious?" And with that being said, they laughed together and hugged one another. He told her in the most convincing voice he could, "I promise with all my heart, baby."

THE FOLLOWING MORNING, ANGELO WAS UP BRIGHT AND EARLY at six AM. He looked over at Asia and saw her resting comfortable underneath the satin sheets. He didn't bother waking her because he had some business to take care of. He went into the bathroom and got himself together, and within the next hour, he was driving through the Houston streets in a white Tesla with dark tinted windows. He looked at the clock on the dashboard, it read seven fifty-three. He dialed a number on his iPhone and a female's voice came through from the other end.

"Hey baby, you back in town?"

Angelo had one hand on the steering wheel and checking the rearview at the same time. He spoke out inside the car. "Yeah, I'm here for a minute. What you up to?"

"Shit, just woke up," the lady said from the other end. "Are you coming through for a minute?"

"Yes, but I'm telling you now that I don't have time to lay up and all that shit," Angelo said in a serious tone. He was changing lanes now; the Houston city traffic was getting thick in the early morning.

"I'm offended."

Angelo smiled; he knew the lady on the other end was going to say something like that in response. "Listen to me real quick, Dominique."

"Nigga, I don't wanna hear that shit…"

CLICK!

I know this bitch didn't hang up in my face, he thought. He looked at the screen of his phone, stared at it for a brief moment, and tossed it in the passenger seat. For the rest of ride, he rode in silence and thought about his blueprint that he had in his head. His main thing was that he didn't want to mess up his new beginning with him and Asia.

For the next twenty minutes, Angelo weaved in and out of traffic until he arrived at a two-story gray stucco home that was surrounded with an electric wrought iron fence. Angelo punched in the security code at the gate and within seconds, the entrance parted open. He pulled the Tesla up the winding driveway until he got to the front of the house. When he put the car in park and switched it off, the front door came open, and as he was stepping out. He noticed the chick Dominique was standing there in a short silk robe that was open and exposing the front of her naked body.

I just told this bitch... he thought as he was closing the door and walking up the steps to the front door. When he made his way to her, he paused at the threshold, just in front of her.

"You gonna stand there or let me in," he said to her.

Dominique was a short red woman with a nice body, jet-black wavy hair, slanted eyes and attitude that was a little too much for Angelo at times. She rolled her eyes and turned her back to him and began walking through the foyer. Angelo walked in and closed the door behind him. He followed her through the marble foyer and into the dining room and on into the kitchen. Dominique went to the table and sat down. Angelo didn't follow her any further. She looked at him. Then she put one leg up on the chair and spread her legs. She touched the lips of her vagina and said to him, "So, my pussy don't interest you anymore?" Then she inserted her middle finger inside of her.

Angelo was looking dead in her eyes as he leaned against the wall, crossed his feet, and held the most serious facial expression that she'd ever seen. "Go get my money," was all he said. He folded his arms across his chest, as if she was on a time clock. Dominique looked at him for at least thirty seconds until she realized that he wasn't budging. Once again, she displayed her sassy attitude as she stood up.

"Nigga, a real bitch can always tell when it's another bitch involved," she said as she was walking off. Angelo sat down at the table as she was heading up the stairs. When she got to the top, he heard her cursing underneath her breath and then he heard the door slam shut. Angelo looked up and let out a slight laugh, shaking his head from side to side as he checked his messages on his phone. A moment later, he heard the door upstairs push open and slam against the wall. That caught his attention; he stood to his feet and walked to the bottom of the stairs as she was coming down. Dominique was carrying a black nylon duffel bag. When she finally got to the bottom of the stairs, she had no choice but to stop directly in front of Angelo.

She handed him the bag. He gripped the straps of it and just stood there, staring at her.

At one point, Dominique was Angelo's girlfriend; they'd been in and out of their relationship for the last three years. Even though he'd bought her the house that she was living in and had actually put her on her feet by investing into a nail shop for her, Dominique was indeed grateful for it. However, with her attitude and mentality, she couldn't respect the fact that Angelo was a hustler and a businessman. And he had nothing but mostly females working for him.

"Thank you," he told her, then he turned around and headed to the front door. He turned back around and looked at her before he walked out. "Don't play yourself out of position. You *can* be replaced." He turned and left, just as fast as he arrived. By the time he was back inside the car, his phone rung. He looked down at it. Asia's name was attached to it. As he was pulling out of the driveway, he answered.

"Hey."

"Good morning," Asia said from the other end. "Just wanted to call you."

Angelo was out into the street now. "I'm glad you did, I'm heading back that way, but I have to make another stop first."

"Okay, I'm here. And guess what?"

"What?" Angelo responded.

"I talked to my Dad this morning. He actually apologized to me. I couldn't believe it."

"That's really good news," Angelo said, then he asked her, "Did you tell him to go get your car from the airport?"

"No, why would I do that?" she asked.

"Because, I think you'll look better in something else," he said, and went silent. He wanted to hear what she was going to say to that. Angelo was sharp and definitely on top of his game. His phone buzzed with another call. "Hold that thought, let me take this call." And without waiting for a response, he clicked over to the other line.

"My boy. What's good with you," he said into the car, speaking in the speakers.

"Aye, everything is good on this end," the guy said from the other end. "How about them Dallas Mavericks though? That boy Luka Dončić dropped twenty points the other night."

Angelo knew that was the code for twenty keys of cocaine and that they needed to be delivered to Dallas Texas as soon as possible.

He responded, "Man, you know I'm a Houston Rockets fan for life. But since you keep talking about that boy Luka, I'm coming to the next home game. Just have my front row tickets."

"Front row, all Houston fans have to sit in the nosebleed section." He laughed.

Angelo laughed along with him. They exchanged a few more words and then they disconnected the call. Angelo drove in silence for the next few minutes. He was thinking about the money. He dialed Dominique's number. The phone rung several times before going to voicemail. That made him feel some type of way. He dialed the number again.

No answer.

Just then, Angelo got off on the next exit and turned around and headed back to her house; he'd became angry just that fast. As he rode in silence, he thought about his situation, and he was ready to go beat Dominque up. At least, that's what was running through his mind at the moment. As he rode, he decided to call Asia back and let her know that he was going to be a little late. She told him that she understood and that it wasn't a problem. They stayed on the phone together the whole time until Angelo pulled back up at the entrance gate of the house. When he was punching in the security code, he said to Asia, "Let me call you back." Then he hung up just as the gates were opening. He pulled up to the door again, got out, and went up the steps. Dominique would have normally been at the door by now. He punched in the code on the front door keypad, and it made a humming sound. Angelo was getting angrier by the minute as he walked in.

"Dominique," he yelled out, directing his voice upstairs.

No response.

Angelo walked upstairs and started calling her name as he went. He went towards the master bedroom; the French doors were slightly parted open. He pushed the door open and walked in. There, he noticed Dominique laying in the middle of the bed naked with a needle wedged in her neck, her eyes weren't all the way closed, but she was near death. She'd overdosed on heroin. Again. Angelo just stood there and shook his head.

Stoopid ass bitch! Was all he could say as he rushed to the bed. He got on his phone and dialed a number, as he looked at her in pure disgust.

CHAPTER 8

*T*HIRTY MINUTES PASSED, and by now, Angelo had removed the needle from Dominique's neck, trashed it, and carried her to the bathroom where he'd placed her inside the jacuzzi tub filled with cold water. She was completely naked, and she was slowly gaining conscious again. He lifted her eyelids with his fingers, moved his face close to hers, and stared in her pupils.

"You with me?" he asked her.

Dominique slowly nodded her head up and down. Then her lips moved. "I'm sorry."

"It's okay. But I'm gonna take you to get some help." He moved away from her, but he sat on the side of the Jacuzzi tub. He watched her splash water on her face until she started to cry.

"I'm alright," she finally said. Her eyes looked up at him.

Angelo stood up, walked toward the bedroom, and left her there. "Get dressed," he said to her when he strolled back to the bathroom door before walking back into the bedroom and then downstairs to the main floor where the kitchen was. He sat down at the table for a minute and thought, *I got to get this dope down here to Dallas.* He was trying to figure it out, but

Dominique was his driver; and of course, he was fucking her, but she'd turned to a heroin user. And now at this point, he was through with her. Angelo didn't trust too many people; he'd been crossed by friends and family members over the course of the last few years. Then an idea hit him; he got up and went back upstairs to one of the three guest rooms. Inside, he went into the walk-in closet and closed the door behind him. The closet was filled with clothes, women shoes, and several suitcases that were neatly stacked up. Angelo got down on his knees and moved a few of the boxes out of the way. He found a small button underneath the wooden case. He pressed it, and the wall panel moved up about twelve inches. There in his hidden stash spot, he pulled out a huge duffel bag and looked at it before he unzipped it. Inside was solid bricks of money that was wrapped in rubber bands and clear plastic wrap. Angelo pulled each one from the bag one at a time. On each one of them, he had the amount written in red magic marker.

100K

75K

100K

90K

55K

75K

100K

75K

That was the last one, and it was all there, just as he'd left it. Now it was time to move it because he wasn't going to keep taking chances with it being there. This was the last straw with Dominique, and he meant it. After he loaded the money back into the bag and zipped it up, he closed the stash spot and lifted up the bag and pulled it onto his shoulder. Angelo walked back downstairs. This time, he was moving a little faster than he was when he went up.

Downstairs, he walked outside and put the bag of money in

the front trunk of the Tesla and closed it down. When he walked around to the driver side of the car, he saw Big Moe pulling up at the entrance gate. He was driving a Sprinter van that had *Roadside Assistance* across the front and a one eight hundred number that went with it. Angelo walked out to the fence as Big Moe was sticking his head out the window.

"You need me to come in the gate?" he asked.

"Nah, stay there," Angelo said. "I'm coming out." He went out the gate through the walkway and went up to the driver side window. "Listen," he said in a low tone to Big Moe. "I need to take the van. You gonna have to get the Tesla, but first, I need to get the money out. I need you to take Dominique's ass downtown to the drug rehab and check her in. Leave her there. I'll call you later."

"I can do that," Big Moe said, and stepped out, leaving the Sprinter van running and giving Angelo some dap. Then he asked, "Is anything in the house?"

"It's clean," Angelo said. He then walked over to the car and got both bags of money and went back to the Sprinter van. Angelo didn't waste any time tossing both bags in the back of the van, then he bounced in the front seat. Before he closed the door, he called out to Big Moe. "Aye, she naked in there. Don't let her trick you," he said, smiling and put the van in reverse. He saw Big Moe throw up the thumb sign and kept walking toward the front of the house. Angelo was short on time, so he knew he had to get his work down to Dallas as soon as possible, and he needed a driver. He got his iPhone out and dialed his sister's number. She answered on the second ring.

"Hello," she said from the other end.

"Kat, what's good on yo' end," he asked.

"Shit, just sittin' up here smokin' me one," she said. "What's good with you?"

Angelo paused for a moment and thought about the desperation move that he was about to make. He did a lot of things and made a lot of mistakes in the past by not going with his first mind. Then he said, "I was just calling and checking in with you."

"Nigga stop playin', you know damn well I know you by now. What you need?" she asked him.

Angelo didn't say anything at first; he was watching the road and collecting his thoughts. Then he said to his sister, "Man, shit just crazy. This chick Dominique tripping." He left it at that. Then she came back with a quick question.

"Brah, why are you still dealin' with that chick?"

Angelo pressed his lips together and slowly shook his head. "It's over with this time, sis. I believe I got me a *real one* this time."

"Yeah yeah," she said, then added, "If she from Houston, you dead." She started laughing from the other end.

Angelo laughed with her, then they talked some more, and he told her about Asia from top to bottom. Angelo finally got off the phone with his sister, and then he dialed Asia's number. She answered with a melody tone of voice.

"Hey."

"Hey babe. Just wanted to let you know that I'm five minutes away from you. I'm going to come in for a few minutes and then I have to take a trip."

Asia paused for a minute. Then she said. "Is it a solo trip or can I come with you?"

Angelo got silent for a moment, slowing up as he came to a red light. A text message came through his phone. He looked down at it and it was from Asia. He opened it while the light was still red. It was nothing more than twenty-five red heart emojis and the face blowing kisses. Asia had a way of making Angelo smile, and he was loving every minute of it. He said to her. "If I wasn't driving, I would respond to your text message."

The light turned green, so he pressed on the gas and rode. "Do you wanna ride with me," he asked her.

"Of course," she said. "I'm a rider."

"Say less then," Angelo said.

By the time Angelo arrived at the apartment, the smell of scrambled eggs, turkey sausages, and grits were floating up through his nostrils. He walked in with the two duffel bags on each of his shoulders. Asia met him at the door, raised up on her tippy toes, and kissed him. "You cooked breakfast?" he asked her.

"Yes. And I have your plate ready," she said to him.

Angelo turned around and closed the door and locked it. He began walking toward the second bedroom and as he went, he said, "Okay, give me second." He went into the bedroom, closing the door behind him. The room was neatly decorated in all black and gray. There was a king- sized bed equipped with a secret compartment, and he was the only person that knew about it. He grabbed the remote from the nightstand and pressed the power button. Then he began pressing the volume button up and the top of the bed slowly begin to rise. Inside the bottom of the bed was a built-in steel box that had more cash inside. He unzipped the bags and carefully removed the money from them and loaded up the box, stuffing it in carefully and neatly. After he'd got everything situated, he went back out and into the kitchen area. Angelo washed his hands at the sink as Asia was coming out of the bedroom. He noticed that she was dressed in a tight-fitting jogging suit that enhanced her curves. Before he sat down, he looked her up and down.

"Damn! You look good," he said, and meant it.

Asia took his compliment with a smile, and she walked up to him. "I haven't felt this good in all my life."

Angelo hugged her. "Don't make me put today on pause," he said to her.

Asia grabbed his hand and pulled him toward the table where the food was sitting. "It's probably a little cold, let me put it in the microwave." She took the plate and waked over to the microwave and heated it up. While Angelo waited, he sent out text messages. He knew he needed to make another stop before he and Asia got on the road. It didn't take him long to eat; he was on the clock now because he was about to do something that he normally didn't do, delivering several kilos of cocaine to Dallas.

Angelo packed a light carry bag and so did Asia, and they were downstairs and inside the Sprinter van within minutes. Angelo drove across town and within thirty minutes, he was pulling up into a commercial business complex, one of his own buildings that he was renting. This was where his roadside assistance company was located. There were four Sprinter vans parked out front. All of them were his and had the same name, title, and logo displayed on them. He and Asia got out of the van that they were in. He locked it up and they walked over to another one. He unlocked it and they got inside. In this particular van, Angelo had a secret compartment built in the floor where he'd had the cocaine already inside. He started the engine, looked over at Asia. "You ready?" he asked her.

She looked at him. "I'm ready," she responded. And at that point, she didn't have a clue what she was doing or getting herself into.

* * *

FROM HOUSTON TO DALLAS, IT TOOK THEM ABOUT THREE AND A half hours to drive. During their trip, Asia and Angelo talked about goals and life. Neither of them had kids, and that was rare, especially for Angelo. He was thirty-one years old, but he was on a mission to be rich and happy.

However, from Asia's standpoint, she never desired to be rich, and she never desired to be married to a drug dealer, or even a hustler. She wanted to be somebody's wife and she explained that to Angelo. She was different to him and he was different to her. But they agreed with one another that they would try their best to move forward, regardless of whatever they were faced with.

Angelo arrived in a McDonald's parking lot where he noticed a black Mercedes G Wagon with tinted windows parked in the rear, as if it was broken down. Angelo pulled in the front of it, nose to nose. A tall slim dark-skinned guy in designer jeans, a tee shirt, and off-white sneakers stepped out. Angelo got out of the van, shook the guy's hand, and they exchanged a few words. In the next few minutes, Angelo and Asia were in the G Wagon, and the slim guy was driving the Sprinter Van. They went their separate ways. The work was delivered, and Angelo had the money stashed away inside the G Wagon. He looked over at Asia, and she was looking down at her iPhone doing something. "You hungry," he asked her.

Asia looked up at him, smirking a little. "A little bit," she said. Then she finally looked around inside of the G Wagon. "I can drive if you want me too."

Angelo wasn't really tired; he was charged up and full of energy. "I can use a break. I'm gonna stop at Chic-fil-A and we can switch seats in the parking lot."

A little after eight o'clock that same night, Angelo and Asia was home and sitting at the kitchen table, sipping Dom Pérignon Vintage from champagne glasses. They were both in a relaxed mode. Angelo was clad in a pair of comfortable linen pajama pants, no shirt or shoes. And Asia was in a pair of skimpy gray shorts and a matching wife beater. She had a natural sex appeal about herself, from the top of her head down to her toes. She picked up her champagne glass and brought it up to her lips, the whole time she was looking at Angelo. Then out of the blue, she asked him, "So, why did we switch cars?"

Angelo wasn't ready for that question, not after all this time. *Here we go with the questions,* he thought. He had to pick up his glass and take a sip before he found the perfect answer.

"Honestly, I didn't know if you wanted a SUV or a car. So, since you had a chance to drive the G Wagon, do you like it?"

Asia had a confused look on her face. She was caught off guard with that answer and question. "You lost me, baby," she said to him, sipping on her second glass, and she was starting to feel it a little.

"The G Wagon," he said. "I got it for you. Or if it's too big, I can get you a car." He had a straight face as he gave her the best lie that he could come up with.

"Angelo, are you serious right now? Like for real?" she asked him, as if she couldn't believe what she was hearing.

Angelo reached over and grabbed her hand. He said in a soft deep voice, "Asia, I don't think you took me serious when I said I *want* you, and I want you *here* with me." He carefully rubbed the back of her hand. Staring in her eyes, he saw she was at a loss for words, and he didn't say another word to her. They just looked at one another for a few minutes.

"Sometimes, it just be so hard to trust after all the pain," she told him.

"Fuck the word *trust*, I'll just have to *show and prove*. Now, I'm not about to sit up here and tell you that I'm in love and all that fake shit. We'll have to allow that to come with timing, okay?"

"See what I mean," she said, and allowed a deep breath to follow. Then she went on. "It's one thing to talk a woman out of their panties, but you done talked me out of my heart." She sipped from her champagne glass again, and then they both laughed at her comment.

"Well, I guess we back at *trust* again," he said, laughing.

Asia shook her head with a wide bright smile on her lips. She stared at him; she was filled with joy inside and out. *So, when are we going to get married,* she wanted to say.

"What are you thinking about," he asked her. His eyes squinted as if he knew she was thinking about something that he couldn't figure out.

"Nothing really," was all she said.

Angelo twisted his mouth in one corner and allowed a silly expression to play over his face. "Now you know I know better."

Asia turned up her glass again, then she sat it down with a *clink* against the table. She looked straight at Angelo and said. "Okay, you really wanna know? Falling in love, being happily married, having a big house with a pool, and maybe about four kids. Two girls and two boys. Or somewhere in the vicinity."

For a long moment, Angelo just looked at her. Now holding his champagne glass with both hands, his eyes went to the table, then he looked back up at her. He finally said, "We both desire some of the same things. Except I always wanted like four sons. All by the same woman."

"So, why you never had any kids?"

"For many reasons, one is because I was heavy in the streets and never had a chance to settle down. Two, when I was thirteen years old, I remember one of my uncles owed some Mexicans a lot of money and he couldn't pay them. Then my cousin Deon, who was his son, was kidnapped and was never found. Still to this day, he's never been found. Everybody in our family said it was because my uncle didn't pay the Mexicans. Deon was two years younger than me, and he was like my best friend. So, you know, the same ole story. My uncle gets on heroin and crack, his wife left him, he lost everything."

Asia was looking at him as if she was watching a horror film, her eyes were fixed dead on Angelo. He finally said, "I didn't want any kids because I wouldn't know what to do if that was to happen to me." He turned up his glass and killed the rest of the champagne that was in it. Then he stood up. "I really didn't want to share that part of my life with you. But since we're together now, why not?" He then stepped away from the table because he was actually in an emotional state of mind right now. Angelo walked away and headed toward the bathroom.

When Asia heard the door close, all she could do was look in

71

the direction that he'd went. Tears came to her eyes as she thought of the story that he'd just told her. That alone made her feel a deep emotional love for Angelo; she saw the hurt in his eyes. That was a different type of pain. And all she wanted to do was help him deal with it.

CHAPTER 9

*T*HE FOLLOWING MORNING, Angelo woke up to the sound of his alarm clock that was on his phone. He moved his arm from underneath the sheets, reached over on the nightstand, and hit the stop button on the screen. Asia woke up when he did. She stirred and turned toward him; she was half asleep but somehow still managed to smile at him. He leaned over and kissed her. "I got a flight to catch," he said as he was getting out of the bed.

Asia looked confused, then she propped up on her elbows. "Okay," was all she said.

Angelo worked his way up out of the bed and looked at his phone, noticing that he had a few missed messages. Before he opened the first one, he looked over at Asia. "I'll be back in a couple of days, but while I'm gone, I want you to get with my sister... she's going to show you around H-Town, places where you can get your nails, feet, hair, and whatever else you need."

Asia sat up and nodded her head in agreement, she wasn't really the get all dolled-up type. But hey, why not? "Okay. Are you gonna give me her number," she asked.

Angelo was looking at the message from his right-hand man

Big Moe: **Brah, Dominique went crazy. They admitted her into the crazy house.**

Angelo's face balled up a little, he was confused. He responded back to Big Moe: **What the fuck she got going on?**

Big Moe responded back: **No idea brah, I just know she started talking about spaceships was following her. Then she started punching at the air in front of the doctors. From there, they wanted her to get checked. And they kept her.**

Angelo couldn't believe what he was hearing right now. He shook his head as he stared at the text message. Then he replied: **Okay, I'll take care of it from here.**

Big Moe: **Say less. Keep me posted and hit me if you need me.**

Angelo looked up from the phone and found Asia staring at him.

"You didn't hear nothing I said."

Angelo sat down on the side of the bed, and then he leaned over toward her, his face two inches away from hers. "My bad, what did you say?"

"Are you going to give me her number or is she going to call me?"

Angelo pulled up his sister's number, took a screenshot of it, and sent it to Asia's phone. "I just sent you her number," he told her. "Just let her know who you are and you can go from there." He gave her a quick peck before he went into the closet, grabbed something to put on, and within the next fifteen minutes, he was gone.

ASIA LAID IN THE BED FOR A FEW MINUTES. SHE WAS IN DEEP thought again, something that was starting to happen every day at this point. She moved the sheets away from her body and stood up, stretching and flexing her arms above her head. Asia walked into the bathroom and looked at herself in the wall mirror. *So far, so good,* she thought as she stared at her reflection. After she got herself together, she went around the apartment and cleaned up, vacuumed, and got the entire kitchen spotless. When she did sit down, she was out on the balcony, enjoying the fresh air and the scenery. She was now dressed in skintight denim shorts, a white halter-top, and bedroom slippers. Just looking out into the clear blue skies, smiling to herself. *Am I dreaming or what?* She allowed the thought to play around in her head. Then for some reason, she thought about her furniture that was still in the apartment back in Augusta. At that moment, she got her iPhone out and called the manager of the apartment building. A strong older woman's voice came through the phone from the other end.

"Ridge Way Apartments."

"Good morning, my name is Asia Armstrong, and I'm calling to see if I can have an extension on my apartment and getting everything out."

"Hold on for a second, hun," the lady said from the other end.

"Okay," Asia said, now standing up. The phone was in her hand and on speaker.

The lady came back on. "So, what I'm seeing as of now, you were already evicted."

Asia's face turned into a frown. "What? You can't be serious right now."

There was a long silence from the other end. Then the lady said, "Ma'am, I'm not sure if you read the contract. But there was a shooting in your apartment. And one of our tenants got shot. The owner had your things removed two days ago when nobody answered the door."

Asia stood there frozen, looking at her phone in disbelief. She couldn't believe what she was hearing. And without another word, she ended the call and sat down on the patio chair. "I don't believe this shit." She said in a low tone, the words barley escaping her lips. Asia sat back and allowed her body to slump, placing her phone on her lap and closing her eyes for a few minutes.

Deep breathe, she said herself, and then followed her own instructions and took a few deep breaths and counted as she went. She found herself very relaxed at the moment. However, something in the back of her mind was telling her that she needed to go back home. Not just because of the furniture, but something was tugging at her mind, heart, and soul. That was a feeling that Asia had been dealing with all of her life. At that moment, she picked up her iPhone and dialed Angelo because he knew all the right answers. The call didn't go through because she had an incoming call that stopped it. Asia didn't know the number, but something told her to answer it anyway.

"Hello," she said.

"Hey, Asia, right?" The female's voice came from the other end. Then she said. "This Kat, I'm Angelo's sister."

Asia smiled with relief. "Oh, hey Kat," she said in an up-tempo voice.

"Look, we 'bout to hook up as soon as I get these bad ass kids down to this day care center. But I got one minor problem. I got to drop my car off to get serviced. Will you be able to pick me up from there?"

"Of course, just send me the address, and let me know what time I need to be there," Asia responded. She had a hint of excitement in her voice now. She stood to her feet.

"Give me a few minutes, I'm about to send it to you in a text," Kat replied back. "Go ahead and get ready, Asia." Then she hung up.

Asia looked at the phone, slightly laughed at the end of the conversation, and walked back inside with a little more pep in her step. And in the next fifteen minutes, she was downstairs walking through the lobby and strutting like she owned the place. When she got outside, she saw the black G-Wagon parked about twenty feet away from her. It was backed in, sitting high, and looking mean. She had the key chain in her hand. When she unlocked the doors, the headlamps blinked. Then she got to the driver's side, opened the door, and climbed up and got in. *Damn, I feel like I've arrived,* she said to herself as she looked around and admired the interior. Asia pulled down the visor, popped her lips in the mirror, and started the V-12 engine. She felt the power from her hands to her feet. She looked at the address in her phone and put it into the maps on the dashboard. Then Asia had to do one more thing before she pulled off. She went to her playlist and found the song *Bodak Yellow* by Cardi B, and before she could put the truck in drive, she was feeling herself. When the first words that came from her mouth as she sung along with the song, she had NuNu in mind. *"Said lil bitch, you can't fuck with me if you wanted to. These is red bottoms; these is bloody shoes."* Then she rode off, following the GPS and listening to her music all the way until she got to her destination.

Asia rode through Houston as if she'd been there before, moving in and out of traffic. Despite the heavy traffic, she finally pulled up in the parking lot of Porsche of West Houston. Asia instantly pressed on the brakes and slowed down. She noticed a woman standing in front of the all-glass showroom floor window waving at her. Asia knew it had to be Kat; she was dressed in tight fitting jeans that were ripped on both thighs and knee area. She couldn't make out the logo on her shirt, but she noticed the red and white Givenchy sneakers she was wearing.

Kat walked up to the passenger side door and without warning, she opened the door and climbed up. Asia had a bright smile spread across her face as she looked at Kat. She was indeed pretty, smooth creamy brown skin, her lips were thick and glossy. Asia couldn't see her eyes because she was wearing Cartier shades. Other than that, her nails were done in several different colors, and her weave was bone straight and down the front of her shoulders. Kat was looking at Asia also, and the first thing she said after she closed the door was, "Damn you pretty." And she meant it.

Asia blushed. "Me? You're gorgeous."

"Girl look, we got a lot of pretty bitches and boss niggas down here in Houston," she said. "But when I get you to the right people, hair, nails, lashes... watch how Angelo start keepin' yo ass home." She laughed.

Asia laughed with her, putting the G-Wagon in drive. "I need an upgrade."

"Shiiiiddd, you with my brother, he's one of the riches niggas in Houston. You upgraded when he brought you down here. That nigga so picky when it comes to women. I swear."

Asia gave a silent sigh. She definitely needed to hear that. Then she asked Kat, "Where we going first?"

Kat was holding her iPhone in her hand, looking at the screen for a second. She looked at Asia and said, "Third Ward, I got a Brazilian homegirl over there that will do your nails, brows, and lashes. From there, we'll figure something out."

* * *

LATER THAT NIGHT, ASIA AND KAT BOTH WERE DOLLED UP. SHE'D taken Asia all over Houston. Now they were sitting in a half circle leather booth in a nice elegant restaurant. The table was round and covered with a clean white tablecloth. Just after they had been seated, Kat ordered two shots of 1942 Don Julio Tequila with no chaser and a glass of red wine. The waiter arrived with the drinks. He was a handsome Italian guy that was dressed in black pants and a crisp white button up shirt. He sat one shot in front of Asia and the other one in front of Kat. "Thank you." Kat said to him with a smile.

He bowed his head with respect. Then he sat the glass of red wine down in front of her as well. "Enjoy ladies. I'll be back in a few to check on you," he said before walking away. Asia picked up her shot glass and sniffed it. Then she frowned. "Wow, this smells strong."

Just then, Kat picked up her glass. She held it out to Asia, and they clinked the glasses against one another. "To success and prosperity," she said.

"Success and prosperity it is," Asia agreed, then she turned up her glass in one swift kill. Kat did the same thing and that was that.

Kat sat her glass down and looked at Asia. "Truth be told, I don't be out too often like this. Angelo wanted me to show you around the city. Something I barely do is mingle with people that he has in his circle because his choice of selection for women is..." She paused and caught herself.

Asia said, "I understand." Finishing the sentence for her.

Kat nodded her head, then she smiled and said, "That forty-two so smooth, it'll creep up on you." Then she asked Asia. "You got any kids?"

Asia smiled. "Not yet."

Kat laughed and held up her open palm hand. "I hear you girl."

Asia gave her a high five and they laughed and joked for the next hour or so. By the time Asia had gotten home, it was almost one o'clock in the morning. When she stepped through the door, she flipped on the light switch and found that the entire living room was covered with dozens and dozens of red roses, candles were lined up around the room, and the ceiling was covered with balloons. Asia couldn't believe her eyes as she stared around. She could barely walk across the floor as she smiled, shaking her head as she walked through. She was so overwhelmed that she forgot to close the door behind her. She turned around and went back to the front door and closed it.

Locked it.

She turned back around again and saw Angelo standing in

the doorway of the bedroom, draped in a black and gold Versace robe. "Now I told Kat to be sure that you got home around eleven," he said with a smile.

Asia nearly ran across the room and jumped into his arms. They hugged and all she did was say, "I wanna be with you for the rest of my life." Then she cried in his arms for the next few minutes until Angelo carried her to the bed, stripped her naked, and they had sex. They carried on like savages for the rest of the night.

CHAPTER 10

*T*HREE MONTHS LATER, Asia had been on the move, smuggling kilos of cocaine, pounds of heroin and methamphetamines from Texas to Mississippi, Tennessee, New Orleans, and all other cities throughout Texas. And the thing about it all, she thought that she was only delivering cars for Angelo's car lots and picking them up from the auctions in other cities.

It was now night, and she'd just arrived back in Houston from a long, one-day trip from San Antonio. She'd delivered only money this time. Just a little under two hundred thousand dollars. Asia was tired, to the point where she could barely keep her eyes open. She finally parked the rental car in one of the empty parking spaces in front of the apartment building. She looked at the time on the face of her phone just before she opened the door. It was ten thirty-seven PM. She shook her head, opened the door, and stood out next to the car. The night air was cool and fresh, and it tossed her hair a little bit. She finally closed the door and headed through the lobby and upstairs to her apartment. When she made it to the elevator, her phone chimed; she flipped it over while she waited for the elevator to come down. She looked down at the screen. It was a text from an unknown number. Asia opened it, and just as she started reading it, the doors parted open. Asia walked inside the elevator and punched the number for her floor.

Sean told me to tell you hello, were the words that came from the text message. Asia looked confused, now she was wondering who in the hell was texting her. She texted back: **Sean who?**

The elevator came to a halt and the doors parted. She walked out and down the hall. By the time she arrived at the door of her apartment and unlocked it, another text message came through. **Damn! You done forgot about a nigga already?**

Asia's heart fell into her stomach, she felt her chest tighten a little. *Is this dude out,* she asked herself, and then she went in and closed the door. Sean gave her anxiety; at least that's how she was feeling anytime she heard his name. She flipped on the lights, sat her purse down on the sofa. She walked straight to the bedroom and turned on the lights. The bed was untouched and crisp, just like she'd left it. Angelo was out in California for a couple of days, but she wanted to be sure because he was so full of surprises. She finally sat down on the bed, still looking at the phone. She was eager to see if it was really Sean. She began typing: **Where are you?**

She took a deep breath as she waited for his response. A few minutes passed and she didn't get anything; she finally stood up. Her mind was spinning in circles. She was slowly becoming worried. Asia began to undress, and as usual, she gathered up her clothes and sat them on the bed. She was down to her leopard print panties and matching bra. She looked at her phone again.

Nothing.

Asia walked into the bathroom, slid the shower door open, and turned on the shower to let it warm up a little before she got in. She walked over to her sink and sat her phone down on the granite countertop. She stared at herself in the mirror and wiped her face with her hands. Another deep breathe, as if she was suffering from asthma. Hot water, cold water. She began brushing her teeth and thinking, *I can't go for it. And why in the hell am I still feeling some type of way about this dude?* She shook her head. "Not this time, Sean," she said as she was looking at herself in the mirror. Asia caught that epiphany and came up out of it just that quick. After she rinsed her mouth, she picked up her phone and blocked that number without any hesitation.

No deal was her thought before stepping into the shower. She got herself together quickly. Once she was finished with her shower, she got out and wrapped herself in Terri cloth robe, tied the belt around her waist and went into the kitchen and straight for the mini bar. Asia poured herself a glass of Dom Pérignon. For a minute, she stood there and just looked at the glass. Then she finally lifted it up to her lips and took a casual sip.

Then another one, this time it was more like a gulp. She sat the glass down and got her phone, going to Instagram and unblocking Nu Nu's page, just to see what she had going on. And the first post that she noticed from her page read: **FML**, which meant Fuck My Life. Asia then went to the next post. And there was Nu Nu, taking a selfie right in front of the county jail on Phinzey Road. Asia shook her head at how bad she was looking now. But the caption read: **Just left Bae, he on the way home with a million dollar lawsuit on the city of Augusta.**

A million dollar lawsuit, she said to herself. Then she took another sip from her glass and sat it down on the table. Asia strolled a couple more pictures. She stopped at a screenshot photo that was blurry and couldn't really make it out. But the caption read: **In due time bitches. Stop hatin'.**

Asia smiled, then she laughed a little and said underneath her breath, "Who hating on you, lil ugly?" Afterwards, she logged out of Instagram and went back to the bathroom and freshened up just before she got in the bed.

Her phone rang. She looked down at the screen. She turned over on her stomach and answered it. "Hello."

"Asia." The female's voice came from the other end as if it was a question.

Asia paused, her eyebrows bunched together, and out of curiosity she said. "Who's calling?"

"You gonna see soon, bitch!"

CLICK!

Asia got a little nervous. She went to her call log and screenshotted the number that just called her. She turned on the lights and dialed the number back. It rung a few times and then it said something about a Google voice. She hung up, and again, she blocked the number. And just then, she decided that it was indeed time for her to get a new phone number. When Asia tried to go to sleep, she found herself tossing and turning. After fifteen minutes passed, she got her phone and called Angelo's number. But he didn't answer, and that was strange because he always answered her call. She then went to the next number that she had for him and that one went straight to voicemail.

Now she was starting to get a little worried. She moved the sheets from her legs and sat up in bed with her phone in her hand. She dialed both numbers again and again, and she still came up empty. *Where the fuck are you, Angelo,* she questioned. Then she stood up. She called his sister's number, the phone rung several times and then the same thing. "The mailbox is full." She hung up. Walking into the living room and flipping on the light switch, she felt herself starting to sweat a little. Asia wiped her forehead; at the moment she didn't know what to do. Now sitting on the couch, she took a chance and dialed Angelo's number again, this time, someone answered. It was a deep man's voice that she'd never heard before. "Who are you looking for," the voice asked from the other end.

Asia swallowed, she didn't know what to say or think at the moment. "I...must have the wrong number." She stammered over her words, and just as she was about to hang up, the man spoke again.

"Angelo's dead, bitch. And we coming to get the money and you next. Stay tuned."

CLICK!

"Ohmygod!" she said, her eyes stretched wide with fear. She stood to her feet, she was so nervous. Not knowing which way to turn, her heart was pumping out of control. Asia hurried back to the bedroom and as she went, she dialed Kat's number again. Still no answer. Then out of nowhere, she heard talking and laughing, but it was Angelo's voice.

Asia finally pulled her eyes open, she looked around the bedroom, and the sunlight was coming in from the thin slit in the curtains. Asia looked at the bedroom door as it was coming open. Angelo walked in.

"I woke you up," he asked her.

Asia had to blink her eyes several times and look around the room. She sat all the way up, bewildered and out of it. Then she said in a low voice, "I just had a crazy ass dream." She got up out the bed as Angelo was moving toward her. He stood on the side of the bed where she was sitting. He put his arms around her neck and she hugged him around his waist.

"Well, I'm here now," he whispered to her. He pulled her up so he could hold her even tighter. Asia laid her head on his chest and just stood there in silence. She didn't want to share what her dream was because she didn't want to speak it into the atmosphere. However, it had her frightened to the point that she was in tears.

When Angelo heard her crying, he pulled back from her and looked her in her face. "What's wrong, baby?"

Asia placed her head back on his chest and whispered, "Nothing." They stood silent for a moment, Angelo rubbing his hand up and down the center of her back. He knew something was going on with her, he didn't want to push it, but he couldn't just let it go like that. He lifted her face and pulled her lips to his until they kissed for a moment. Angelo pulled away from Asia to stare her in her eyes. "I have a minor issue that I need to discuss with you," he said in a calm voice.

Asia felt butterflies in her stomach; she couldn't deal with anything that had *minor issues* in the sentence. She tilted her head back and braced herself. With tears in her eyes, it seemed as if she blew heat from her nostrils. "What is it, Angelo?" she asked in a sad voice.

Angelo pulled her close to his body, they were pressed tightly together. He looked in her eyes. She was looking in his. Then he said, "I need to take you somewhere." He then gave her peck on her cheek. "Hurry up and get dressed." He turned around and headed back into the living room, where Big Moe was sitting on the loveseat watching an old boxing match of Mike Tyson on ESPN. But the volume was muted.

He looked up at Angelo when he entered. "Everything okay, boss?"

Angelo sat down on the sofa next to him. He nodded his head and pulled out his phone, and then he looked at Big Moe. "She said she had a bad dream that had her crying."

"Yeah, I kind of heard her. Not being in your business or nothing," Big Moe said.

Angelo took a deep breath, pulling his eyes from his phone and looking over at Big Moe. "Three more months in this year. After this year, I'm through with this shit."

Big Moe had round buckeyes that were always bloodshot red. He had fleshy jowls and a thick neck that was covered with hair bumps. When he turned his attention to Angelo after that statement, he looked like a wild animal. "Shiiiddd, you gonna put me in position?"

Angelo wasn't expecting that question. But he didn't want to go through the motion of going back and forward with him as to why he think he should leave the game with him; he felt a ping in the bottom of his stomach. Like a nervous feeling that he'd had before. His eyes met Big Moe. "Damn right," he said, then he added. "Who else is gonna handle it?"

Big Moe gave an overwhelming smile, his head slowly moving up and down.

The bedroom door came open and Asia came out. She was dressed in sweatpants, a cute shirt, and pink Nikes. She smiled. "I'm ready." Then she said, "Hello, Moe." She walked over to him, leaned down and gave him a hug.

Angelo stood up, so did Big Moe. "Hey, Asia," he said, and hugged her back.

Angelo looked at Asia then headed toward the front door. "You got your keys," he asked her.

Today, Asia wasn't carrying a bag or anything. She had her keys and iPhone in her hands, but she looked again to be sure. "Yes."

"Okay, because I need you to go to this address." He handed her a folded piece of paper.

Asia took it, unfolded it, and looked down at it. She read it and looked back up at Angelo. "What's these numbers on the bottom," she asked.

"The access gate code. It's the same code to the front door." He then leaned down, kissed her lips, more of a lip-to-lip touch. "Call me when you get there." Then he looked at Big Moe. "You ready?"

Big Moe nodded and walked past Asia and went out the door. Angelo turned and walked out behind him, and Asia just stood there for a moment, appearing to be lost. But she just wasn't feeling the right vibe from Angelo. She slightly shrugged her shoulders and walked out into the hallway and locked the door behind her. Then she felt something wash over her, as if weights were in her stomach. She paused, frowned, and then rubbed her stomach. Asia proceeded walking until she arrived at the elevator.

Downstairs, she made it outside, then to her G Wagon. From there, she hopped inside and put in her location. Before she pulled the SUV in drive, she shook her head in disgust and thought about the dream that she had. *Get it out of your head,* she said to herself. Asia got her music going and loaded in her address. And for the next forty minutes, she rode through traffic and sung along with some of her favorite artists.

Asia finally pulled up to a nice luxurious neighborhood. She couldn't believe her eyes at the beautiful manicured golf course that was at the entrance. As she rode further into the neighborhood, there were huge estates on each side of the street. Asia was turning her head from side to side as she came to a stop at a four way. The GPS told her to turn left. There were two kids zipping by on their bicycles and that made her slow down. She made the left and cruised down a winding street that was lined with more huge expensive homes.

"Turn left in point two miles," the GPS voice said.

Asia was driving even slower this time, and then she came to an immaculate home that seemed to sit thirty yards away from the main street. She turned in the driveway and stopped at the keypad on her left; she looked at the piece of paper and punched in the code that Angelo had given her. When she pressed the enter button, the wrought iron gate opened. She pulled into the driveway that made a circle up toward the front doors. Asia put the G Wagon in park and then she dialed Angelo's number.

"Hey baby," he said.

"Hey, I'm here."

"Have you been inside?" he asked.

"No, I'm in the driveway," Asia responded.

"Well, go inside and take a look around," he said with a light hint of authority in his voice from the other end of the phone.

Asia sat still for a moment as his voice vibrated through the speakers of the G Wagon. She rolled her eyes a little, then she took a breath and said. "Okay." She ended the call, switched off the engine, and got out. When she closed the door and walked around to the front of the SUV, she paused and looked at the front of the home. From where she stood, she examined the twelve-foot French doors. The front of the porch was surrounded with manicured shrubby and pine straw. Asia climbed the steps and punched in the security code on the lock pad. The green light flashed and an air pressure sound hissed and the door came open. Asia walked in and the first thing that she noticed was the glossy white marble floors that led to the white marble circular stairs with black railing. She looked up, the ceilings were high and there was a crystal chandelier that hung directly over her head. Asia closed the door, turned around, and began walking through the empty house. She went toward the den area, where a huge floor to ceiling window stared back at her. She looked out the window and saw a huge swimming pool with an attached Jacuzzi. A gazebo was to the left. For a moment, she stared out the window. Then she pulled out her phone and dialed Angelo's number. When he answered, he asked, "How do it look?"

"The house?"

"Nah. The mailbox, Asia," he said, trying to be funny. Then he said. "Listen baby. These people are selling this house, and I wanted you to take a look at it first before it goes on the market."

Asia hated that gut feeling, but the feeling she was getting right now was a tingle from the top of her head down to the bottom of her feet. She closed her eyes and raised her head up toward the ceiling for a second. "Why do you always do this, Angelo?" She asked in a tone of voice that was low and soft.

"Cause, I love you," he responded in a calm voice. "And my goal is to make you my wife. Now let me know if that house big enough to hold us and our future family."

Asia couldn't believe what she was hearing.

Butterflies.

Heart beats.

Lips shaking nervously.

Moist eyes, then the tears pushed from the back of her eyes so fast that she dropped her iPhone.

CHAPTER 11

*B*Y FOUR O'CLOCK the next evening, Asia was guiding the delivery truck driver through the entrance gates of her new estate. She was standing in the front yard, rocking her Gucci shades, jean shorts, and a long Houston Rockets jersey with Angelo's name across the back with the number 1 on it. When the truck stopped, two Mexicans hopped down from the front. The driver came around and introduced himself. He was wearing khaki pants, boots, and a beige shirt.

"Hello, I have your sofa and TV," he said in broken English. "Show me where you want."

Asia smiled, turned around, and said, "Follow me." She walked through the front door and the two Mexicans were walking behind her. Asia led them to the den area. "Right here," she told him and waved her hand. She turned and faced them.

The round face Mexican nodded his head, and then he looked at his friend and said something in Spanish. The other one nodded and they both headed back outside. Asia walked upstairs to the master bedroom suite, the room was spacious and bone empty. There were separate his and hers walk-in closets. Asia had never seen anything as big as this, except on TV.

Her closet was the size of a small bedroom. She was imagining all her shoes and clothes filling the room; this was like a dream that came true and she was enjoying every bit of it.

Within the next two hours, another furniture company had pulled up with the bedroom set, one that she'd picked out herself. She was so overwhelmed with everything that she decided to call her mother. She reached for her phone in her back pocket and realized that it wasn't there. Then she'd remembered that she left it downstairs. Asia left the room and walked back downstairs. Her phone was sitting on the floor next to a Chic-fil-A bag that she had at lunchtime. She got it from the floor and dialed her mother's number on Facetime. Asia was smiling before her mother answered. She knew that she would be proud of her and all of her accomplishments. Her mother answered, and she had a look on her face as if she was tired. "Hey, Asia."

"Hey, Mom," she responded back cheerfully. Then she said, "Wait a minute, I got something to show you." Asia flipped the camera screen around. She held up the phone as if she was taking pictures or something. "I got a new house."

"Oh, that's beautiful," her mother responded. "Is it in your name?"

Asia looked at the phone, but her mother couldn't see her face. *Why the fuck you have to be so negative,* she thought and made a twisted and ugly face toward the phone. Then she flipped the camera around. "Not yet, Mom."

"Well, it's not your house, Asia." Now they were looking at one another and she asked, "When are you coming home?"

Asia had a simple response. "I am home, I'll come visit soon though. I'm getting this furniture moved in right now. I really just wanted to show you..."

Her mother cut her off in mid-sentence. "Asia, are you pregnant?"

Asia frowned. "Pregnant? Oh my God. No, I'm not pregnant," she said with a smile. "Why would you ask that?"

"I'm just looking at how fat your face has gotten."

"It's just the new iPhone camera. They make everything look big."

"Well, go take the test anyway to be on the safe side," her mother responded. But she kept her eyes glued on Asia as if she was looking deep into her soul. Then she said. "You pregnant. Look at yo' titties."

Asia looked down at her breasts; she wasn't wearing a bra underneath her Houston jersey. And now as she was looking at them, she could see how plump they had become. Asia turned her head back up to the phone. "Never positive with you," she said to her mother. "Talk to you later." Then she ended the call. Now she had something else to worry about until she'd find out if she was pregnant or not. Asia couldn't do nothing but shake her head. She then walked out to the front of the house to see what the furniture guys were doing. Asia saw the Mexicans pulling the last piece of the couch from the truck. It was wrapped tight and neatly with plastic and paper. They were moving very carefully as they pulled it down. She got her phone and googled the nearest Walgreens or CVS, and just her luck, one of them was five minutes away. Asia walked out the gate and went to her G Wagon that was parked in front of the house. She got in and went straight the Walgreens. She was trying to keep her composer, but her mind and heart were racing. It didn't take her five minutes to run into the store to grab the home pregnancy test kit. Then another five minutes to get back home. By the time Asia went to one of the bathrooms upstairs and sat down on the toilet, she was pouring sweat, as if she'd been running from the police. She sat down on the toilet, peed on the stick and sat there staring it for what seemed like two hours.

The plus sign appeared and she nearly fainted.

* * *

WHEN ANGELO PULLED UP TO THE HOUSE, IT WAS SEVEN O' THREE and the sun was setting and giving off a beautiful orange sky. He was driving one of the Sprinter vans. When he stepped out, he looked like an automotive mechanic. His Dickie suit was covered with dried oil and stains. He had his phone up against his ear and seemed to be pissed at someone from the other end. When he got to the front door, Asia opened it before he could. She wrapped her arms around him and stopped him in his tracks.

"Baby, you ain't gonna believe...."

Angelo held his finger up to her and shut her down. Then he said into the phone, "So, a hundred thousand just vanish and don't nobody know nothing?" He walked into the living room and just stood there looking at the floor with his hand over his forehead. Angelo was beyond angry, at least that's the way Asia was looking at it. She overheard the conversation and couldn't believe what she was hearing as well. She calmly pushed the door shut. Then she stood there for a minute to see if Angelo was going to look at her.

He didn't. She understood his frustration, but she wanted to tell him the good the news. She walked in the den and sat down on the brand new Italian leather sofa and looked at her phone until he was off of his.

Then she heard him say, "Brah, I'm not about to accept no lost on a careless ass nigga. That shit don't have anything to do with me, my girl delivered."

Asia cocked her head slightly, and then everything had gotten silent. She couldn't see Angelo, but she could hear him, especially when he said, *his girl delivered*. She looked back at her iPhone and went to Instagram. The first thing that came across her timeline was a post from the Shade room. Asia hadn't been on in so long that she felt as if she was out of the loop on things.

Puff Daddy was in the news. Bill Cosby was in the news. Lil Wayne was in the news. Flat tummy tea was in the news. Fashion Nova was in the news. Then she clicked on the website and started shopping. For the next ten minutes, Asia felt as if she was about to have a mental breakdown. But she'd had that feeling before and it wasn't a good one.

"Just get my motha' fuckin' money." She heard Angelo scream this as he was coming around the corner. He was coming straight towards her with a facial expression that she'd never seen on him before. "Look. Short notice. I'm about to go to San Antonio."

Asia stood up and put her arms around him. "Please baby, just calm down for a minute," she said.

Angelo hugged her, kissed her, and then he pulled away from her and looked her dead in her eyes. "I got to go handle this business," he said.

"Angelo, I swear I had a dream that you got hurt. Please stay home with me." She was nearly in tears as her words flowed from her mouth.

Angelo gave her a sinister smirk. "That wasn't a dream, baby." He kissed her. "I'll call you when I get there." He tried turning to leave, but Asia was still holding onto his hand. He looked down at her with a look as if to be saying, *let me go.*

Asia caught the stare, she wasn't about to put herself through this; she let go of his hand, and he turned and walked away from her and headed out the door. When Asia heard the door shut, she slowly walked into the foyer and stood in the bay window of the dining room. She watched Angelo go out to his Sprinter, and as he was getting inside, she couldn't help but allow the tears to flow down her face. *Dear God, just please cover him and protect him. That's all I ask.*

The following morning, Asia got up early. It was almost seven AM when the doorbell rang. She knew that the first delivery for the dining room table and appliances wouldn't be there until ten. She got her phone, pulled up the ADT app and looked at the doorbell camera. There was a lady at the front door. She was wearing shades and carrying a nylon backpack. Asia noticed that her hair was pulled back in a ponytail. Asia pressed an icon and asked, "How can I help you?"

Asia saw the lady's face in the camera, and it appeared as if she was saying something, but she couldn't hear her. She got up out the bed, and then grabbed her mace gun. She was sleeping in her panties and a thin tee shirt, so Asia quickly slipped on her shorts and headed down the stairs. When she got to the door, she didn't open it; instead she said from the inside. "Good morning. The audio isn't working on the doorbell."

The lady said from the outside, "First of all, this *is* my house. Who the fuck is you?"

Asia was caught off guard with *that* statement to the point that she had to check herself to see if this was real or another damn dream. *Your house? Now this isn't how I intended to start my day,* she said to herself.

"Ma'am. I think you have the wrong address," Asia said through the door.

"Listen, I'm not sure who you are, but my name is Dominique Albright. I was admitted into a drug rehab a few months back. This *is* my house. All my shit is still in there."

Asia was nearly laughing now; she couldn't believe what she was hearing. Not this early in the morning. Asia didn't know if she needed to call the police or Angelo. She took a deep breath, and then she said carefully, "Ma'am, I just moved in here yesterday. My boyfriend literally just purchased this house."

"Your boyfriend?" she shouted. "I hope his name isn't Angelo. If so, honey we got a lot to talk about."

There was that feeling in her gut again, only this time, Asia felt her knees buckle. Right then, she froze and just looked at the door. *This shit can't be happening, not now.* Asia's hand went to the lock, twisting it until it clicked. Then she opened the right side of the French door. She looked at Dominique, and they stared one another in the eyes for a moment. Then Asia stepped to the side and said, "Come in."

When Dominique stepped across the threshold of the front door, she looked around inside the foyer and the floors. "You mean to tell me this nigga changed the floors and everything," she said, then her eyes went to Asia. She extended her hand. "I'm sorry for my rudeness. I didn't catch your name."

Asia paused for a moment, and then she extended her hand. "I'm Asia."

Dominique gave a half of a smile. She was mad as all outdoors. "So, I guess I should start off."

Asia nodded, then turned and headed into the den. Dominique followed behind her and they sat down together. "Listen, baby girl. I'm not tryin' to ruin what you and Angelo got going on. But I *literally* was just livin' here in this same house four months ago. I used to fuck with Angelo's dog ass. Excuse my language."

Asia's stomach was twisting in knots now, the hot flashes were coming and going, tiny beads of sweat had begun to form on her forehead. She looked at the floor and then back at Dominique. "Just let me know the facts," she told her.

Dominique sat on the edge of the sofa. Her legs were open. "Okay, the nigga had me messed up. I'm sure you know, but I was used to be his main mule."

"Mule! What is that?" Asia said, confused.

"A Mule is someone that move the dope. I was his go-to bitch, like a down ass bitch that will go to Mexico or to Cali or anywhere to get the dope or drop it off, using them Sprinter vans. But see, I messed around and start using the shit. That's when I really lost him. But he had me staying here in this big ass house. Well, a small house compared to the one he has in San Antonio..." She fanned her hand, then went on. "But that's another story."

Asia blinked her eyes and held up her hand. "Wait. What did you say? The house in San Antonio?"

Dominique stretched her eyes and looked at Asia. "So, you mean to tell me you don't know 'bout his wife and kids in San Antonio?" She twisted her mouth. "He really got you in the blind."

At that point, Asia's throat got dry. She knew the lady that was sitting right here in the same room had to be lying. "I know for a fact that he don't have any kids because his sister told me."

"His sista? That lyin' ass bitch Kat?" Dominique let out a loud goofy laugh so hard that her head went backwards.

For the next hour, Asia talked, but she listened more than anything and she was so hurt that she didn't know which way to turn at this point. While Dominique sat there on the couch next to her, she pulled out her phone and dialed Angelo's number, but he didn't pick up. She held the phone right there in her hands and cried.

Dominique touched her hand. She said, "Shit, if I was you... I'd take all that nigga's money and go back to Georgia." She held an unlit Newport between her lips.

Asia just sobbed and shook her head; she didn't want to hear that. She just wanted all this to be a lie or a dream. Anything except the truth. Then her phone rung. She looked at it. It was Angelo calling. When she slid the green button to the side all she could do was say, "So, you been playing me all this fucking time, Angelo?"

"What the fuck is you talking about now, Asia?" he asked in a disgusted tone of voice.

"I'm up here carrying your baby and you got a whole family."

"Asia, you trippin', baby. Where is you getting this information from?"

"From your side bitch, Dominique... that's sitting right here with me. The lady who was just living in this same house before me."

Angelo sucked his teeth from the other end of the phone. "That bitch a heroin junkie. You can't believe shit that she says. I'm calling Big Moe; he'll be there in a minute."

Asia's tears were flowing now. Her chest was rising and falling so hard that it seemed as if she was about to faint. "So, you haven't been having me trafficking drugs for you?"

"Hell no. Don't believe that bitch," he screamed. "Put her ass on the phone."

Just then, Dominique heard him yelling. She screamed out, "Fuck you nigga, I don't wanna talk." She stood up, her face screwed up with anger.

Asia looked up at her as if she didn't want her to leave. Dominique picked up her bag. "Sorry for the inconvenience," She said, and then she turned and walked out. "Ahk-ki-ki," she laughed as she went.

Asia stood up and went to the door and saw that Dominique was gone down to the bottom of the driveaway. Then she said into the phone. "I...I...just...I'm done."

There was a long pause. "Let me call you back." Then he hung up.

Asia tossed her iPhone on the small table that sat in the corner; luckily it didn't break this time. She bit on her bottom lip, hugged herself, and just cried like a baby. Asia was lost and caught up in her emotions. She grabbed her iPhone and went upstairs to the bedroom and laid across the bed on her stomach. Her eyes were puffy, and she was beginning to feel nauseated. *This shit can't be happening.* Asia got up just in time as she felt herself about to vomit. As she was heading to the bathroom, she made it to the sink and threw up. "Awwww." She made that sound as her stomach was closing and caving in. "Agggg." She felt as if she was choking now. Asia turned on the water in the sink and stayed there, bent slightly at the waist for what seemed like forever. She looked down at her shirt and noticed that she'd gotten vomit on it. She took it off and tried to wash it in the sink because all of her clothes were still at the apartment. Then her phone rung. She tried her best to wash her face and rinse out her mouth to remove the nasty taste. Asia went back to the bed where her phone was at. She picked it up and answered it.

"Have you calmed down yet?" Angelo asked her.

Asia froze, twisted her head to one side as if she couldn't believe what she was hearing. "Are you serious right now, Angelo?"

"Look, I didn't have you delivering anything. So you can get that bullshit out your head for one. Next, if you gonna let this sour ass junkie disrupt what we got going, you're crazy."

"Tell me the truth, Angelo," she said.

"I just did. Now, do you want to come down here to San Antonio with me and see for yourself?" He sounded so calm, smooth, and convincing.

Asia wiped her eyes with the back of her hand, she was sniffing and sobbing. Confused, angry, and in love. "I don't know what I wanna do," she finally said.

"Okay, well at least I tried." Then he hung up the phone in her face.

Asia looked at the face of her phone, and when she saw that he'd actually hung up in her face, she couldn't believe it. *"Fuck you, Angelo. Fuck you...Fuck you...And fuck you,"* she yelled angrily at the phone. She was beyond pissed now; she went back into the bathroom and turned on the shower. Then she remembered that she didn't have any underwear. *Yes, I do.* She said to herself; she had a bag downstairs in her G Wagon. Asia went downstairs to the kitchen and out the garage door. Her G Wagon was parked inside. She opened the rear passenger door and grabbed her duffel bag that she had with a change of underwear. And as soon as she closed the door and was about to go back inside, the garage door started to roll up. Asia paused and turned around as the daylight was coming in from the spacious door.

Big Moe was standing there, along with two other mean

looking guys. Big Moe walked all the way inside the garage while the other two stood there as if they were waiting for something. "Asia, what up," he said as he got closer to her. The bottom of his shoes were scraping against the concrete floor.

Asia was looking him up and down as if she was saying, *What?*

"What the hell you and Angelo got going on?"

"Nigga, don't play crazy with me… you already know cause you down with the bullshit," she said in a nasty tone, her eyes and neck rolled at the same time.

Big Moe snickered and shrugged his shoulders. "Well, okay."

"Well okay, what," she snapped.

"Well okay, he sent me over here to get you out of the house," he said in a nonchalant tone of voice.

"Get me out the house?" she yelled and nearly laughed, "You got me fucked up, and I'm not about to go anywhere." Then she turned around and walked back inside the house. She had made it to the kitchen by the time Big Moe grabbed her by her wrist and gave her a small yank, just enough to make her stop. She frowned and looked at him, and the look that he had in his eyes was cold and intimidating.

Then he said, "Call him, *now.*"

Asia freed up her wrist and dialed Angelo's number on Facetime; she wanted him to see what the hell his friend or uncle or whoever was doing to her.

When his face appeared on the screen of the phone, Angelo was holding a little light skinned boy with curly hair. He sat him down and said to the little boy, "Go play with your brother, daddy will be there in a minute." He then looked at Asia. "I'll assume Big Moe is there. Give him the keys to the G Wagon and the keys to the apartment. He's gonna give you two thousand dollars, and he's about to take you to the Greyhound bus station. The next bus to Georgia leaves in two hours, and that's how long you *have* to be out of Texas."

"What... Are you serious?" she said. Her face was twisted up and her heart was thumping so fast that she felt as if she was about to have a heart attack.

Angelo hung the phone up, and once again, she looked at it in disbelief. She finally looked up at Big Moe. "Can I go to the apartment to get my clothes first," she asked him.

"Angelo said he bought all the clothes, baby. I'm sorry. My orders are to take you straight to the bus station and to make sure that you got your ticket."

"Well, can I at least take a shower first?"

He shook his head. "It's not my call sweetheart," was all he said.

CHAPTER 12

*W*ithin an hour, Asia's entire life went from sugar to shit. She was in one of the rows of chairs at the Houston Greyhound bus station with her elbows on her knees and her face buried in her hands. The noise was all around her, people chanting about something that was on the CNN News channel. At this point, she felt defeated, lost, unloved. And with so much mental pain going on with her, she felt she didn't have anything else to live for.

Her bus ticket was set to go to Atlanta and then to Augusta. But she couldn't allow her parents to see her like this. *Not like this.* Tears were running, streaming down her face through the cracks of her fingers and slowly dripping to the concrete ground beneath her. She sniffed, wiped her face with her hands, but she didn't look up. For the next few minutes, she sat still until her tears dried up on their own. Then without warning, she sat up and crossed her legs. Her lips were pressed tightly together. Asia scanned around the inside of the bus station. There were a crew on Mexicans sitting across from her, two men, a woman and baby that didn't appear to be no more than four or five months old. When she saw the baby that sent her swirling right back into depressed mode. *I can't believe I'm carrying this dude's baby, and he gave me his natural black ass to kiss. That's what yo ass get.* She tried laughing it off, but the pain that she was enduring right now was unbearable. Just to the right of her, a slim white woman sat down next to her. Asia cut her eyes briefly in her direction and then she smelled the stinking cigarette smoke that was coming from her mouth and clothes. Asia didn't say one word, she grabbed her small bag that she had and stood up; she still had about another forty minutes before her bus was departing. She turned and walked outside underneath the breezeway and got some fresh air. She watched the cars pass by, transit buses, and homeless people walk the street. Asia put her back against the wall and pulled out her iPhone, she didn't have anything else going on. No text messages, no missed calls.

She then decided to call Angelo's number. She was blocked. That was something that she just couldn't believe. Then out of nowhere, a homeless couple was coming up, the man was unshaved and unkept; he was pushing a grocery store shopping cart that was filled with black trash bags. The lady was in the same shape, her hair was nappy, and her lips were chapped. Asia dropped her head and looked at her phone again in hopes that they wouldn't stop. Then she heard the woman say. "Look at how pretty she is, Thomas."

Thomas was the man's name. He was looking at Asia; he had on dirty gloves with the fingertips cut out. Asia looked up, and then she smiled and said, "Hello."

"All we need is two dollas," the lady said, her eyes were dead on Asia.

"I only have a twenty-dollar bill," Asia told her. "If you want that, you can get it." Then she dug in her front pocket of her shorts, allowing her fingers to only slip one of the top bills from what she had in there. When she pulled it out, she handed it to the lady.

"I only need two," she said.

Then Thomas chimed in. "Bessie, just take the damn twenty."

Bessie turned her head and looked at Thomas, her face was still and cold at the same time. When he caught the stare that he'd seen so many times before, he politely turned his head and the buggy toward the left and got quiet. The older lady, Bessie, looked back at Asia. Then she moved a little closer toward her and in a low whisper, she said to Asia, "Thirty-seven years I been wit' this damn fool and he still dumb as a box of rocks." She laughed and flashed a set of uneven and yellow teeth. "But I guess dat' make me a bigger fool."

Asia had to laugh with her. Then she nearly forced the twenty dollars in her hand. Bessie took it. "With this, yo' blessings will come one hundred times ova'," she said, and then she leaned down, rolled up her right pants leg, and tucked the bill in her sock. But before she stood up, she pulled out a small glass jar that was no bigger than sample cologne bottle. She stood up and twisted off the top. Bessie poured some of whatever was inside of it in the palm of her hands and put the top back on it. She then looked at Asia. "Gimme yo' hands," she demanded.

Asia put out both of her hands and Bessie grabbed them and squeezed them tightly. "Look at me," she told Asia.

Asia was looking around, hoping she wasn't about to get robbed or anything. Then she looked Bessie dead in her eyes. "The pain that you goin' through is only tempa' rerry. From dis' day on, you will be blessed, yo kids will be blessed." She squeezed her hands tighter and shook them. "All you got to dew is ask for what you want." Then she let Asia hands go and stepped away from her. "God has his hands all ova you."

Asia looked at her with a long-lost stare. Then she said, "Thank you." Asia turned and headed back inside of the bus station. As she walked, she couldn't do anything but think. *Where did that conversation come into play at?* She slowly shook her head as she went to find her a seat.

When a lady's voice came over the intercom to let her know that her bus was boarding, she looked up at the digital signs. Seventeen hours on the bus was something she didn't want, but she didn't have a choice. Now she was hoping that she could find a good seat and that it wouldn't be too packed.

Asia was the fourth person on the bus, and she went closer to the rear just in case she needed to use the bathroom; she found a window seat on her left, four rows in front of the bathroom. Asia had her bag, her phone, and a bottle of spring water. She went in her pocket and pulled out her ear pods; she didn't have a cordless charger for them, but she was going to use them until they went dead. The bus was filling up fast, but everyone wasn't going to Georgia, some of them were going to Louisiana and Alabama before they got there. Then some were just going. Just like her. Asia was just going; she hadn't made up her mind yet, but she wasn't going to her mother and father. *Not like this.*

This is a nightmare. This can't be real life. She thought about everything again and wiped her face with her hands. She turned and looked out the window, it seemed like a typical day in Houston. People were walking by, some were standing outside talking with their friends that had come to pick them up from the bus station. While she was lost in thought and looking out the window, she heard the voice of a fast-talking Mexican and she looked up at him. He walked past her with a ball cap pulled down over his forehead, and the female Spanish lady was just behind him; she was carrying the baby on her shoulder and she was drop dead beautiful. She made eye contact with Asia and smiled at her and nodded her head, maybe it was beauty recognizing beauty. Asia smiled, and then she dangled her fingers a little. The both of them sat together and Asia looked down at her phone screen; she opened the text message icon, and to her surprise, she saw that her mother had sent her a text thirty-five minutes ago. Asia opened it and it read: **Regardless of how you feel about me, just know that I'm praying for you every**

**morning when I wake up and every night before I go to
sleep. Love ya.**

Asia smiled, and then she responded with a line of red heart
emojis. Still, with that being said, she still wasn't about to go in
that direction. Asia rested her head back against the headrest
and closed her eyes for a moment. The bus continued to fill up
quickly. She folded her arms across her chest and tried to just
relax. She drifted off to sleep for what seemed like a few
minutes. However, forty minutes had passed by, and when she
finally woke up, her eyes were facing the window, and she saw
nothing but fields and paved roads passing by. They were on the
road now. She looked to her left where the seat next to her was
now occupied. Asia didn't want to stare at the stranger that was
sitting in the seat next to her, but he had an aura about him. He
didn't look her way when he saw that she'd waken. He was
cleaned shaved with smooth caramel skin; he wore his hair cut
low with shiny waves that were spinning all the way around his
head. Dressed in some cheap looking jeans, a white long sleeve
button down shirt.

In the next moment, he removed his big plastic earphones,
looked at her, and said, "Was I singin' too loud?" He stared her
dead in her eyes.

Asia didn't say anything, she just shook her head from side
to side at him. Then he slipped his earphones back on his ears,
turned his head straight, and closed his eyes. Asia wasn't
impressed, nor was she interested in how he looked. She turned
her head back toward the window and looked, continuing her
ride in silence. Asia sat and thought about what her next move
would be. She didn't have a clue. "I got a little money," she whispered. "I can stay in a motel and get a job. Probably get around
in an Uber..."

"Who you talkin' to shawty," the stranger next to her asked.

Asia looked at him. She was shocked that she was even
talking loud enough for anybody to hear her. "I thought you

were listening to your music." *Why the fuck is he even talking to me? Why are you in my business?* These thoughts were running through her mind.

But the stranger had thoughts of his own. *Shawty, you really lame as hell. Soon as the first available seat comes open, I'm moving away from yo crazy ass.* Out loud he said to her, "I just got them on my ears. My CD playa isn't workin'."

Asia squinted her eyes a little and turned her head slightly to the side. "Wait, your *CD player* isn't working?"

The guy stared at her, then he turned his head, stood up a little, and scanned the rest of the bus in hopes of there being a vacant seat somewhere. There wasn't one. *Somebody needs to swap seats with me,* he thought. He finally sat back down, took a short deep breath, and looked at Asia.

"Yeah, CD PLAYA. The ones that they give you in prison." He shrugged his shoulders.

"Well, that explains it," she commented. "And to answer your question, I was only talking to myself, really trying to figure out my next move."

"So, you not crazy?" he asked her. His face expression never revealed any emotion whatsoever.

Asia rolled her eyes. "Tuh." Then she turned her head back toward the window and shut her eyes. The guy shook his head and turned his head away from her. They rode a few more miles, and the bus was out in the middle of nowhere on a Texas highway when suddenly it seemed to be slowing down. The bus driver's voice came through the speakers. *"Hey, ladies and gentlemen. From what I can see now, we're coming up to an Immigration police checkpoint. They'll probably be coming on board,"* he advised the passengers.

Asia's eyes opened; the guy next to her eyes opened. Several people began waking up and the chatter started low, and then it began to get a little loud. From the isle, the Mexican guy that was sitting across from Asia and the guy next to her looked at the dude that was next to Asia and said, "Hey, my friend."

He removed his earphones and stared at the Mexican that was only inches from his face. "Yeah, what up?"

The Mexican pointed at his own chest. "I no have no papers. My wife no have no papers..." He paused and looked back at his wife and baby, the bus was almost at a complete stop. He then looked back at the guy that was looking at him. He went on. "Please...I no want my wife and son to go back to Mexico." He almost had tears in his eyes.

Then the guy said, "What you need me to do?"

The Mexican said in a near desperate voice, "Please...Sit wit' my wife and baby."

The guy stared at him for a moment, and then he looked over at the Mexican's wife, and she was looking at him and holding the baby. Without warning, he got up and moved across the isle and got in the seat next to the Mexican lady. The Mexican guy got in the seat next to Asia.

The Greyhound bus had finally stopped and the driver opened the door. There were two police officers waiting on the outside of the door as he opened it. Both of them walked aboard, one behind the other, their badges were out. The first one paused at the bus driver; he had a shaved head and a suntan that had his skin red. He flipped his shades down. "It'll only take a minute," he said.

The driver nodded his head and they walked on past him. Both of the officers walked slowly down the middle isle, looking carefully from one side to the other one. There were all races and nationalities on the bus. They were scanning everybody. And by the time they got to the middle of the bus an older looking white man said,

"Yeaaaaahhhh, make America great again." His teeth were raggedy and his breath was stinking. The first officer paused and looked at him. Then the white guy held up both of his middle fingers. "You don't even have the fuckin' right to be on here. Let me see your paperwork."

"Sit down, sir," the first officer said.

"Make me. I fought for this fuckin' country before you were born, son, Master Sergeant E Eight rank." Then he stood up and put his middle finger up in his face. Then without another word, he sat back down. The two officers got further toward the rear of the bus. On their right, they saw a black guy holding a baby up and down in front of his face. "Goo goo...gaaa gaaa." He was making baby sounds with his mouth and the baby was smiling and laughing as he was going up and down in the air. Next to him, the Mexican lady was playing sleep; she was curled up against the window, and on her head was a red and white cap that read: **Make America Great Again.** They looked right past them, and as they were about to turn around and leave, they saw the Mexican guy sitting next to Asia. They stopped. Looked at him. Then, the shaved head police asked him, "Can I see your ID?" He was standing over him and looking down at him.

The Mexican knew his wife and baby was in the clear, but he wasn't ready to go back to Mexico at all at this point. Especially from everything that he'd just went through to get this far. He tucked his lip underneath his teeth and cursed himself. He couldn't even look at his son and wife to say goodbye, so without saying anything, he stood up, turned his palms face up, pressed his wrist next to one another, and in a low whisper he said, "Me ready...I no have paperwork."

And just like that, they took him and escorted him off the bus without another word being said. Asia swallowed hard, and she looked out of her window and watched as the police escorted the Mexican to the side of the road. He was holding up his arms as they were checking his pants pockets and waistline. They made him kick off his shoes, and then the bus was rolling again. Asia turned her head away from outside and looked over at the stranger that was just sitting next to her. He was still holding the little baby, only now he had the little boy up against his chest, rocking him side to side as if he was a veteran at being a father. Asia smiled, and then she gave him two thumbs up.

He flashed a smile, but he didn't reveal his teeth. His head moved up and down a little and then he leaned over to the Mexican lady that was still playing sleep. He whispered, "They gone."

She moved the hat from her head and face, and when she looked at the stranger, she had tears in her eyes. But a smile came right after that. "No English," she said.

The dude nodded his head and handed her the baby. She got her son back. "Gracias...Muchas gracias mi amigo."

"Say less." He then patted her on the shoulder and went back across the aisle and sat in his seat next to Asia. Asia was looking at him as he sat down. "Wow...God will definitely bless you for that," she told him.

He looked at Asia. "I can use a few blessings right about now," he said, but the way he talked, he never showed his teeth.

"They're coming," Asia said, then she asked, "What's your name?"

"Daquan," was all he said.

"Daquan? Nice, I'm Asia." She put her hand out.

Daquan grabbed her hand firmly. "Asia's a cool name. You must be Chinese or somethin'."

Asia burst out in laughter. "Hell no..."

They were both interrupted by the Mexican lady across the aisle. "Mi amigo...Mi amigo," she said.

Daquan looked over at her and noticed that she was holding an iPhone in her hand. She pushed it over to him. "Speak English..."

At first he gave the lady a strange look as if to say that he didn't want to talk. But he felt Asia nudge him. He looked back at her and she made a face. He turned back around and took the phone from the Mexican lady and put it up to his face. "Hello," he said into the phone.

"Hello, mi amigo," the voice said from the other end. "My sister, she tells me the news, she speaks little English. But you did something for her and she want to say thank you."

Daquan nodded his head and looked at the lady across from him; she was smiling and holding her son for dear life. Then he said into the phone, "How do I say *you're welcome* in Spanish?"

"De nada," Asia said from behind him.

Daquan quickly turned his head and looked at her; he pulled the phone from his face. "Stop ear hustlin'," he said in a joking matter. This time he smiled and revealed his teeth. Asia saw them for the first time and noticed that he was missing one of his front teeth.

She played it off, shrugged her shoulders, and pretended to be looking at something on her phone. The guy from the other end said, "De nada."

Daquan looked at her and said, "De nada." Then he said into the phone, "Okay amigo, good talkin' to you." He handed the Mexican lady the phone and bowed his head a little at her. She got the phone and spoke to her brother for few a more minutes. When she got off the phone with him, she looked back at him. "Mi hermano quiere tu numero."

Daquan looked at Asia and he nudged her with his elbow. "What did she say," he asked her.

Asia looked over at her and asked her to say it again. When she repeated herself, Asia said to him, "She said her brother wants your number."

Daquan said to Asia, "I don't have a phone."

Asia looked at Daquan and shook her head at him. *Hell is your phone?* "Do you want me to give her my number?"

Daquan turned up his lip and curved them down. "I don't care."

Asia got the lady's phone from her and she dialed her

number, and when it rang she answered and locked it in. Asia asked her, "Name?"

The Mexican lady said, "Alejandra."

Asia smiled, then she texted her name to her. She then got up and took her son into the bathroom to change him. Daquan looked over at Asia. "You too friendly, shawty."

"Too friendly, why do you say that," she asked him.

"Cause, I'm jus' sayin'. You just...gullible." He looked at her.

"I know..." Asia said, and her voice drifted off. "I really need to work on that, especially the way I just..." She caught herself and paused, thought about what he just said, and now she was about to put a total stranger in her business.

"See there, you were just about to say somethin' you had no business." He slipped the earphones back on his ears, leaned his back against the headrest, and closed his eyes.

CHAPTER 13

*a*sia stared at him for a moment, wondering why he kept slipping them headphones on his ears. She politely tapped him on his shoulder. Without opening his eyes or looking at her, he said, "What Asia?"

"I need to talk. I got shit on my mind," she said.

Daquan sat for a moment, then he opened one eye and looked at her, releasing a long breathe. "You need a counselor, shawty," he said. "I'm just a street nigga that jus' got out of prison. I been gone six years, so I got my own problems."

"Okay, we both got problems then," Asia said. Her eyes were turning glossy a little bit; she was still looking at Daquan as if he was about to say something else. But he just sat there with his eyes closed for the next few minutes. When Asia finally realized that he wasn't trying to talk, she turned over on her right side and tried to get comfortable. She closed her eyes.

"So now you wanna go to sleep?" Daquan said to her.

Asia sucked her teeth and just shook her head without turning around to look at him. "I'm trying," she finally said.

"I'm from Atlanta," he said, removing his headphones again and turning in her direction. She was still facing the wall window as Daquan started talking to the back of her head. "I'm just kind of…antisocial I guess."

Asia was still facing the window with her eyes closed when she responded, "That's a skill that I need to work on." She was using her hands for pillows.

"I'll help you with it," he said, and then he went on. "So, tell me somethin' 'bout yourself."

Asia paused, nearly frozen for a moment. "I don't even know where to start, my life is some grade A bullshit right now."

"Well, it's not like I don't have time to listen. Where are you goin'?"

"…Atlanta, I'm going to stay in a motel or something until I can get my shit in order."

"You know what's crazy…I'm gonna probably be stayin' in a roomin' house. Come out cheaper than a gettin' a room. My sistah said that I could stay there with her, but nah. I was supposed to have been home last year, but I didn't have nowhere to parole out at, so the state of Texas made me max out." He paused for a second. "But the best part about it… I don't have no paper or parole. I'm free to go where I want."

"I'm free myself, well, until I have my baby," Asia said.

"Damn! So, you pregnant right now?" Daquan asked her.

"Yes, I am," she said, "…and that's what's bothering me." Asia finally turned around and faced Daquan, her eyes weren't wet, but she was staring nearly into his soul.

"Before you get started, let me say somethin' real quick. I don't have no foundation whatsoever. But it's like this, let's see what we can build. I'm not about to tell you nothin' that I can't one hundred percent stand on."

Asia shook her head slowly. "Oh no, I'm not looking for another relationship. Not after all the bullshit that I've been through."

"Let time be the judge, in the meanwhile… let's talk. Then we'll get this shit figured out."

Asia finally smiled. "First question, what happened to your front tooth?"

Daquan smiled, trying to cover it up with his hand, but she'd already seen it. "The night I got locked up out here in Texas, I came with a few so-called homies to an event called South by South West. We got to fightin' with some dudes from another state. We made it to the van that we came in, and when we were heading back to our room, we got pulled over. But we had a gun in the stash spot and they found it. I was the only one that hadn't ever been to jail or nothin', so I took the gun charge and freed everybody. Them red necks in Austin, Texas beat my ass and tried to get me to not take the charge. They knocked out my tooth." Then he held his head up and touched the bottom of his chin. "I had to get twelve stiches right here. I got a fractured rib. Well, I *had* a fractured rib. And after all of that, neither one of my homies that I freed sent me shit." He got silent and shrugged his shoulders, as if it was nothing.

Asia had a look on her face as if she couldn't believe what she was hearing. "That's terrible," was all she could say at the time. "How old were you?"

"Eighteen, five days before my birthday. I'm twenty-five now, I guess you can say I became a grown man in prison."

An hour passed and they were pulling up to a small Greyhound bus station just outside of Louisiana. The driver gave everyone forty-five minutes to grab something to eat, use the bathroom, or whatever else they needed to do. Asia and Daquan got off together. They were in the middle of nowhere, but there was a McDonald's across the street and a gas station next to it. "You hungry?" Asia asked him.

"Yeah."

"Come on, let's go to McDonald's," she said and began walking. They walked side by side across the street. Daquan had a strong structured frame; his legs were solid, like tree trunks. He walked like a wide-legged cowboy, his waist was small, and his upper body was tight and fit, and stood at five feet ten inches tall with long arms. When they both crossed the street reached the McDonald's parking lot, Daquan grabbed her hand when he saw a car coming from their left. He moved her behind him in a quick motion, frowning and holding his hand out. "Slow down lil buddy," he said, and gave a serious look, letting the driver know that he was for real and meant business. From there, he pulled Asia along, and they walked through the side door of the restaurant. When the smell hit Daquan's nostrils, he whispered, "Ba da b aba bah, I'm lovin' it."

Asia let out a laugh that made her look up at him and shake her head. "You crazy for that." She led the way up to one of the open registers. The lady that stood on the other side of the counter flashed a smile. "How may I help you?"

Asia was looking up at the menu; she ordered a salad, a fish sandwich, and a bottle of water. Then she stepped to the side and Daquan stepped up to the counter, already looking up at the menu and rubbing his huge hands together. "One big mac, one quarter pounder with cheese, supersize fries." He paused and looked around. "Let me get two of those apple pies, a large sweet tea, and a bottle of water."

The lady looked up at him after putting in his order. "Anything else," she asked him.

He shook his head. "Nah...That'll be it." He reached in his front pocket, but Asia stopped him.

"Just let me get it this time."

Daquan looked down at her. "Are you sho'? I got a few dollas."

Asia nodded and pulled out two twenty dollars bills and handed them to the lady. After they got their food, they sat down at one of the tables and ate and talked. Then out of the blue, Daquan said, "If I wasn't a changed man, I'd go down to Houston and take every dolla that buddy had." He shook his head and bit down into his big mac. As he chewed, he tried to talk. "I guess that goes back to the sayin' that *everything that looks good, ain't always good.*"

"It's alright, God got me," she told him.

Daquan reached across the table, grabbing both of her hands. "Correction, God got *us.*" He stood up. "Now let's get up out of here before we miss our ride."

Asia didn't even say anything, just stood up with him, and they walked out together. Outside it was starting to get cool and the sun was setting. Daquan was carrying his McDonald's bag with him, and said to Asia as they were crossing the street, "I believe that burger just messed up my stomach."

Asia glanced at him, seeing the look on his face. "Oh God!" she said, smiling. "You might wanna use the bathroom before we get on the road."

Daquan was walking at a fast pace now, most of the people were still standing around; some of them were smoking cigarettes, and she could even smell a strong scent of marijuana in the air. Daquan handed her the bag, and he trotted toward the entrance of the bus. Asia didn't get on; she waited outside and took in some fresh air. She frowned a bit, grabbing her stomach after she felt a little pain at the bottom. It was more of a sharp pinch. Her teeth clenched together for a second. Then the pain was gone. Asia unscrewed the top on her water bottle, turned it up and took a sip, then climbed the steps and got on the bus. When she got to her seat, Daquan was coming out of the bathroom with a smile on his face when he saw her. He sat down next to her, took a deep breath, and rubbed his hands on his knees.

"Let's go see what Atlanta got to offer us," he said.

Asia looked at him and nodded. "And what we can offer Atlanta." She took a deep breath, and then she said a silent prayer. They were on their way.

* * *

IT WAS SEVEN TWENTY THE FOLLOWING MORNING WHEN Asia and Daquan arrived downtown at the Atlanta bus station. Daquan hadn't seen his city in six years. When his feet hit the asphalt, he became overwhelmed. Asia was right behind him, stepping off the bus and examining her surroundings. She pulled up next to him, the wind was whipping through her Houston jersey. "It's cold out here," she said to him.

Daquan put his arm around her and drew her in closer to him. He looked down at her. "I'm gonna give you my shirt and you give me that one, it's always cold downtown in the mornin'."

Asia looked up at him. "How about we just find a Starbucks or something and sit down."

"Coffee and breakfast then?" he suggested.

Good thing Asia did have a few dollars in her bank account. They took an Uber to the nearest Starbucks downtown. Once they got inside, the both of them went straight to the bathroom. And when they came out, they met in line, ordered their coffee, turkey bacon, bagel, and eggs, and they found a seat.

Daquan scanned the many people that were sitting around sipping coffee; some were on their phones and some were lost in their laptop computers. His eyes went to Asia. "Before I met you, my original plan was...I didn't have one." He laughed and sipped his coffee, sitting the cup down.

She laughed. "Before I met you, my original plan was...I'm not sure either. But we really need to go get a room for a couple of days. I need a shower and some clean underwear. Women stuff."

"Asia, before we move forward, are you sure this is somethin' that you wanna do with me?"

Asia gave him a questioning look. "I need to be asking *you* that question. I've heard so many stories about men coming home from prison and going right back," she said. "And the main reason is because of the lack of money and trying to catch up with where they left off."

Daquan moved his head up and down slowly; his eyes were fixed dead on hers. He drummed his fingers on the table as he sat thinking. Then he said, "My old life and friends are dead to me. My grandma raised me; she still stays in the hood, same house. She's the only person that I wanna see. Other than that… it's me and you until the baby is born, then it's us." He shrugged his shoulders.

Asia sat still for a moment and listened at him. For some reason, she seemed to connect and relate with Daquan so good that it was almost scary. She said, "When you go see your grand-mother, will you take me with you?"

"Yes, but I'm not goin' in that area until I get my mind right." He picked up his coffee again and took a sip. Sat the cup back down. Then he said, "I need to get a phone."

"Okay, can we please go get a room so I can shower?" Asia asked.

Daquan nodded and stood, grabbed up the trash, and went to the trashcan. When he came back, Asia was standing and looking at her phone. She looked up at him. "We can get a room at Extended Stay for a week for one hundred dollars. The Uber is on the way."

Daquan agreed. By the time six o'clock came, they had gone to Walmart, got underwear, personal hygiene, soap, toothpaste, deodorant, lotion, mouthwash etc. Daquan grabbed a few t-shirts and cheap jeans. Asia grabbed a few pieces of clothes as well, something that would get her through day to day. They were back in their single room, sharing a queen size bed.

Asia was tired, physically and mentally. She was sitting up in bed, Daquan was next to her, laying on his back with his eyes closed. She looked over at him; he was wearing a pair of grey gym shorts and no shirt. His entire upper body was covered with green ink tattoos. Westside was curved across his muscle ripped stomach, and Angel wings were on his chest with the letters RIP MAMA detailed inside the wings. *His mother must've passed away*, she thought. *I don't even know what the fuck I'm doing here with a total stranger. This is some freaked out desperation shit.* Asia turned her head away from him and softly fell back and laid on the pillow next to him. *This is not happening. Not falling for a dude fresh home from prison that I met on a fucking Greyhound bus.*

DAQUAN HAD HIS EYES CLOSED, BUT HE WAS FAR FROM SLEEP. Over the last three years, he'd found himself meditating a lot. Just as he was doing right now. Then, for some strange reason, he opened his eyes and slowly turned toward Asia. She felt his stir and stare; she turned her head and looked at him. Then he said. "Shawty, I meant Asia..." He paused, and then his eyes began searching her, examining her. He leaned in and kissed her on her forehead, then pulled away from her, staring her in her eyes again. "Why do this seem so strange? Like, if people were watchin'... What would we do?"

Asia propped up on her elbow, moved around a little, trying her best to get comfortable. "Are you some kind of mind reader or something," she asked him. "And my reason for asking is because I was just asking myself, like really questioning myself, about this whole situation."

"Swallow yo' pride and go to Augusta, you still got a mama and daddy," he told her in a low calm voice.

Asia wasn't expecting to hear that. Her eyes turned sad, she was unsure. Trust was a big factor in her life right now. Her eyes were darting from side to side; they were still looking at one another. She said, "I'm all in, Daquan. If I go back to Augusta with a baby, broke, and single..." She paused, felt a lump in her throat.

Daquan reached over and caressed the side of her face with the back of his hand, his touch was warm and smooth. "But you ain't single. I thought we was together now." He smiled.

She reached and held the hand that was against her face. "She too extra, I'm so serious." Then she smiled and let out a laugh. "I really do wanna try this new thing with us..."

"I'm not a thirsty nigga, shawty. Just solid and real. We can stay on our friendship thing if that'll make you comfortable."

"One minute I'm comfortable, the next minute, I'm confused as fuck. I don't want to stress myself to the point where I lose my baby."

"Either we struggle alone, or we can come up together," Daquan told her. "The choice is yours."

Asia fell backwards and covered her face with her hands. She thought about the old lady in Houston at the bus station. *The pain that you goin' through is only tempa' rerry. From dis' day on you will be blessed, yo kids will be blessed.* Those words were in her head like a tattoo. She finally moved her hands and looked at Daquan. "I'm in, I'm all in."

Daquan smiled, leaned close to her, and brushed his lips up against hers. "Good choice. One moe thang. And you don't have to say *nothin'* right now. But, I'm going to marry you. Wait, I didn't say that right. Will you marry me? But don't answer that shit right now 'cause I'm broke and I don't have a ring or nothin'..."

"Yes, just let me know whenever you ready," she said.

"*Damn!* Let me get my weight up first," he responded back with a smile, flashing that missing tooth again.

"I said just let me know whenever you ready."

"Shiiiiddd, we can go to the courthouse and let the judge do it," he said, waiting to see what her response would be.

"If that's what you want, Daquan. I'm ready," she said, but this time she sounded sincere and sure of herself. Asia didn't have anyone to impress, and she was finally realizing that when a person has a vision or dream, you never know how it may come. But it will eventually come if you seek it hard enough.

The following morning, Daquan was up bright and early. It

was five AM, he was still on his prison routine: three hundred sit-ups, three hundred push-ups, and two hundred crunches. He rarely did legs and upper body on the same day. However, since he was in a different place, he was prepared to do different things. He tried his best to stay quiet and not wake Asia, but it was nearly impossible. He stood up, only inches from the foot of the bed. He was bare chest and his muscles were ripped and bulging. When he turned up his bottle of water, he looked at Asia.

She said, "Personal training this morning I see."

Daquan was breathing hard; his face was serious. "I tried not to wake you." Then he got back down in a push-up position and began going up and down in a slow motion. He was focused on what she was doing. Asia moved the sheet and blanket from her body and sat up. She pushed herself to edge of the bed to see what he was doing, and to her surprise, he moved like a machine and the muscles in his back seemed to have been carved and sculpted. *My God,* she thought. Then she stood up and walked around his legs. He stood up and turned toward her. Asia looked up at him, his face was shinny from sweat, his neck and chest was sweating, and his stomach and torso formed into a V shape. "You ever thought about modeling," she asked him.

Daquan shook his head. "Nah, you think I can get on with it?"

"What? Are you serious?" She began rubbing her hands across his chest and down to his stomach. "These are real muscles," she said with a hint of laughter in her voice.

Daquan grabbed both of her hands around her wrist. "As of now, I'm going to get a job, somethin' to get us an income comin' in."

"Have you found somewhere already?" she asked him.

"Not yet, but the way they building up in Atlanta, I'm sure I can walk on one of these construction sites. I don't give a damn if I got to go hold a *slow and stop* sign for minimum wage, we not stayin' here forever."

"Well, while you're out doing that, I need to find me a doctor up here. And you never got a phone, so I think you definitely need to grab you one while you're out." She turned and went to the nightstand and pulled the drawer open. Inside, there was the small amount of cash money that she had. She still had about thirteen hundred in cash. Asia counted off five hundred and gave it to Daquan. "Get what you can with this."

Daquan took the money and nodded his head. He was standing over her, sweat still dripping from his face and body. Asia never moved, just looked up at him. He reached and grabbed her around her waist; this was his first time ever touching her in that manner. He drew her closer to him until his sweaty body was pressed up against her breast and stomach. Her eyes had a sad puppy dog stare. When he leaned down, all he did was pressed his forehead up against hers. "We gonna be alright," he said in a low whisper to her.

Asia couldn't break away from his stare; it was if he'd had some kind of spell on her. Her lips barely moved when she said, "I trust you."

Daquan broke away from her, turned, and said, "Let me shower real quick." He went toward the bathroom, and Asia was still standing there for the next three or four seconds. She finally walked over toward the window; she was in a white halter-top and loose-fitting sleepwear pants with a wide bottom. She moved the curtain open a little, the sight wasn't eye pleasing at all. Just a twelve-foot wall of gray cinder blocks. The room was on the first floor at the back of the hotel. Just standing in that position brought back the memories from Las Vegas and Houston. Even the one-night stay in Miami when she's made a run for Angelo and she stayed overnight at the Fountain Bleu. Daquan turned on the shower; the sound of the water brought her out of her trance. *The only difference between*

Cinderella and me is that my slippers were Christian Louboutin Red Bottoms. And that nigga even took them back. She had to laugh at that herself. She finally turned away from the window, took a few steps toward the bed, and sat down on her side.

Am I really going through a state of depression? She laid back and asked herself that question for the tenth time. *The first boyfriend shoots at me. The second whatever spins my entire world upside down. Now I'm...* She sucked her teeth and again and started crying so hard that it felt like she couldn't even breath. Asia turned over on her stomach, buried her face in the pillow to muffle her moans and her cries. She didn't want Daquan to see her crying. Her chest felt as if it was getting tighter by the second. *My God.* Was all she could say, and as the time went on, her tears were slowly drying up. When she heard the shower stop, she tried to quickly wipe away the leftover tears with the pillowcase. *I can't let him see me like this.* She jumped up from the bed and pressed her legs together and pretended like she had to pee. When Daquan came from around the corner from the bathroom area, she was just about to rush toward him until she saw he was wrapped from the waist down in a thin flimsy terrycloth towel. She stopped, staring down at the bulge that was curving and pressing against the material of the towel. Asia couldn't help herself; she reached and touched it. Then gripped it. Daquan wanted to stop her, but it had been a while since he felt the wet and warmness of the inside of a vagina. She felt it growing in her hand underneath the towel. "Is this real," she asked and smiled.

"Move the towel and see."

Asia didn't even remove the towel from his body; she just opened the split where it was parted and pulled it out. He was big, thick, and hooked. Then Asia tried to close the towel up, but she looked up at him, dead in his eyes. "I got to use the bathroom," she said, and brushed on passed him and closed the door behind her.

Daquan removed the towel and dried himself off and quickly put lotion on his body. He went to the bag where he had his brand new boxer briefs. When he pulled out a pair and removed the thin strip of tape, the toilet flushed. He heard the water in the sink come on and then the door open. When Asia came around the corner, she walked right up to him and stood between his legs. Without any warning whatsoever, she went down on her knees and put him right in her mouth. Starting with the head, she circled her tongue all the way around it, and Daquan moved his legs farther apart. Asia knew what she was doing. At this point in her life, she definitely wasn't a rookie to it. She rolled her eyes up and looked at him. His eyes were nearly closed, and he began shaking and trembling, trying to push her head back.

He came.

And it kept coming like a faucet left open. He reached out and pulled the sheet from the bed to help catch the flood of cum so it wouldn't get on her. His heart was racing uncontrollably. Daquan felt so embarrassed that he couldn't even look at her. "Let me get dressed," he said to her.

Asia didn't say anything, even though she was so hot and her panties were soaked. She finally stood up and watched him go back inside the bathroom. She couldn't help but smile and giggle at that.

That really made her morning.

CHAPTER 14

*T*HREE DAYS LATER, Asia didn't waste any time grabbing a job. She was hired nearly on the spot at a restaurant called Yard House in Atlantic Station as a waitress; she figured that with her and Daquan's situation, she needed to be at a food spot to bring some home for free or to at least grab an employee discount. It was almost six PM when she got back to the motel room and walked inside. The room was clean and straightened up. When she turned the corner, Daquan was sitting on the foot of the bed, removing his work boots. He was dressed in khaki pants and a tank top. He looked up at Asia with a smile and said, "I got the job."

Asia gave a genuine smile and walked over towards him and gave him a hug. "That's wonderful."

"It's entry level, mainly a helper. And I didn't have to go through any bullshit." He said and pulled her closer to her.

"That don't matter, I'm on at the restaurant. So, we're starting and that's all that matters." Asia sat down on his thigh, her arm around his neck, and his arm was around her waist.

"Sound 'bout right," he responded, then added, "What about the doctor appointment?"

"In the morning at nine. It's an OB-GYN clinic right down the street," she told him.

Daquan nodded and rubbed her stomach. "I'm goin' with you."

"What time do you have to be to work in the morning?"

"Soon as I leave the doctor with you," he responded in a smooth and confident voice. He kissed her on the back of her shoulder. This caused her to tense up. She turned to him and rubbed her hands across his shoulders. She hugged him around his neck and whispered, "I don't know what I'd do without you."

Daquan didn't respond, they just held one another and sat in silence.

Asia and Daquan walked in the doctor's office at 8:45 the next morning. The waiting room was warm and comfortable, and the walls were covered with an earth tone color wallpaper. They grabbed two chairs that were separated by a small wooden table that held neatly stacked magazines. Asia got up just as quick as she sat down. She went across the room to the receptionist desk. After she signed in, a pink face lady with blond hair and freckles gave her a stack of forms to fill out. Asia smiled, and then she went and sat down again while Daquan was flipping through a *Home & Garden* magazine.

Trying to pass time, he looked over at Asia as she was starting to fill out the papers that were on the clipboard. "You good?"

Asia looked up at him, nodding up and down. "Just got to fill out all these papers."

"When you get to the father's name, be sure to spell my name correct. Daquan Harrison, okay?"

When he said that, Asia felt her heart stop, and she swallowed, caught off guard. The pen in her hand pressed against the paper. "You want me to put your name down for real," she asked.

Daquan had the most serious expression, but trying to lightened the moment, he stretched his eyes, making a funny face. "Daquan Harrison, woman."

Asia gave the brightest smile that she'd ever given in her life. She looked back at the papers and began to fill them out, saying silently, *Thank you, God.*

* * *

It was a little after one when Daquan walked up on the construction site downtown. The crew was repairing a hole on Peachtree Place, not far from the Southern Company gas building. There was a mini trailer that was sitting on the side for the office. He carried his white hard hat in his left hand, feeling good. He went to the trailer and climbed three steps and knocked on the door.

"Come in," a voice yelled from the other side of the door.

Daquan opened the door and walked inside. There was an older white guy sitting behind a flimsy desk, smashing out a cigarette in a plastic ashtray. "Sorry I'm late, Mr. Wilcox..."

The man behind the desk stopped him in mid-sentence. "You were just hired yesterday, right," he asked him.

Daquan nodded his head. "I was, I had a doctor's appointment with..."

"Listen son, I understand what you saying. But I can't accept excuses from a man that can't handle his responsibilities. Being late on your second day, I'm sorry, Daquan, but I'm gonna have to let you go."

Daquan stood there as if he was buffering, his eyes were dead on Mr. Wilcox. He sat down in the chair that was to his left. "Sir, I understand what you're sayin'. All I'm asking is for you to just hear me out."

Mr. Wilcox's face had turned beet red. He frowned and

stood up; he was stocky with a burley stomach. He suddenly smashed his fist hard against the table in front of him. The ashtray tumbled to the floor. "This is my mother fuckin' business, now get out of here before I call the police."

Daquan was still sitting down; he was so calm that it seemed as if the screaming and yelling and bumping the table didn't faze him at all. He finally stood to his feet and sat the hard hat down on the desk. His face was full of disappointment and despair. "Thanks for the opportunity again, sir." Then he turned and walked out. Down the stairs, he took a deep breath.

The streets were busy downtown. Daquan couldn't believe it. *This shit fucked up!* He punched the palm of his hand as he walked up the street. He removed his orange work vest, tossed it on the ground, and kept moving. Daquan thought about Asia; he hated that he wasn't in a good position. He had his reasons for coming home straight from prison without letting any of his old friends and family members know he was out. But the further he walked, the more he revisited his old life.

When Daquan was fourteen years old, he first jumped off the porch full fledge. Being raised in the heart of crime in an area called The West End, Daquan learned so much from being around the Muslim community. He was never much of a talker; as a matter of fact, the teachers in his middle school didn't want him in their class because he was so silent. And when they tried to reach out to his mother, she never showed up or responded. He was taken away from her because she was a known prostitute and used heroin. Daquan was sent to a boys' group home. He stayed there for two months until he ran away. He then relocated to another rough area that was drug infested and heavy with gang related violence. Daquan was a loner until he linked up with a guy the same age as he was. They were both fifteen, and his new friend had money and his own car. They called him Baby Blue in the streets, but his government name was Marty. He was a bad influence on Daquan, had him doing everything just because he had his own place, money, and a reputation as a known Crip member that would kill you.

Then one night it happened. Baby Blue and Daquan were riding together one night in a brand new Porsche. They stopped at a red light in Old Fourth Ward. Baby Blue was driving and nodding his head to the music that was bumping through the speakers. And just before the light turned green, Daquan swiftly pulled up an automatic handgun that was filled with RIP bullets, also known as Radically Invasion Projectile. Without a word, Daquan squeezed the trigger four times, and Baby Blue's blood splattered all over the car. When his head slumped toward the steering wheel, Daquan flipped his hoodie up on his head and rolled out the car while it cruised; he took off running and never looked back.

His reason for doing it? He was hired to do the job because it was rumored that Baby Blue was playing both sides; he was an informant for the Feds, trying to help his older brother get off of a federal drug and gun charge. After that, Daquan was running with major drug dealers around Atlanta as protection; he never was the drug dealer type, never hung out much, never too flashy or big on material things. And as the months passed, he was asked to go to Austin, Texas with a crew of local rappers. From there, he went to prison.

He brought himself out of his thoughts. Daquan was indeed a changed man now. He wanted better for himself, something different. A wife, a family, a regular job. He jumped on Marta and took a bus back to the motel. And when he got inside, Asia was there, sitting at the small wooden desk; she was on the phone. Her back was to him and she had her head down a little.

"I'm not, dad," he heard her say.

There was a long pause, as if she was listening.

"You're making it sound like I'm just out in the streets selling my body or something."

She got silent again. Daquan moved up behind her and

placed his hands on her shoulders; she jumped a little, turned around, and looked up at him. Asia brought the phone down from her face and pressed the mute button. "He just talking out the side of his neck again," she said to Daquan.

Daquan nodded his head up and down slowly. Then he said to Asia "Can I speak to him?"

That caught Asia off guard. Her eyes gave a questioning look before she looked back at the phone and unmuted it. Then she put it on speaker. "Do you hear me," her dad said through the phone.

"Yes, I hear you, dad." She rolled her eyes.

Then out of the blue, Daquan said, "Hello sir, my name is Daquan. I know you don't know me, but out of respect, Asia is in good hands. I swear to God on that. And I know I'm not supposed to be swearing, but I'm not sure what else to say to get you to believe me or her. We have a baby on the way, and I want to do things the right way. We want to get married and I would like to know…"

CLICK!

Asia looked up at Daquan. "He hung up." She shrugged her shoulders.

Daquan just stood there; he couldn't believe it. He was still looking down at the phone in pure disgust before his eyes went to Asia. "Dad is disrespectful." He went and sat down on the bed and removed his boots.

"Tell me about it," Asia said and walked over to him, tossing her phone on the bed and flopping down on it just behind him. "How was work today?"

Silence.

"I got fired." Daquan turned around and looked at Asia. She turned her head towards him. They stared at one another for a moment.

Then she asked him, "Why, what happened?" She had a concerned look in her eyes.

Daquan shrugged his shoulders lightly, and then he just fell backwards on the bed and laid across her chest. Asia was holding him as she would a baby. "It was because you went to the doctor's office with me, wasn't it?"

"Somethin' like that. But dude didn't even give me a chance to explain my situation." He closed his eyes and got quiet. Asia looked down at him and noticed that a tear was running from the corner of his left eye. Daquan was hurting on the inside, and he was hurting for several reasons. One was that he knew what he was capable of doing. He'd never been disrespected like that since he was a child. Next, all he wanted was to work and to do the right thing.

"Fuck that job," Asia said, and wiped the corner of his eye. Daquan opened his eyes; they were bloodshot red and damp.

"You right, I'll find another one in the morning." He sat up, leaned over, and covered his face with his hands. *You got this. Life comes with ups and downs.*

"In the meantime, I'm going to create you an Instagram page so you can show the world your muscles, talk about your journey, and how you can show everybody else how to get what you have."

Daquan took a deep breath. He raised his head. "You really stuck on that, huh?"

Asia stood up from the bed, walked around, and got in front of Daquan. She placed her hand on her waist. "I know the difference between a fine man and a sexy man, a *fine* man can walk in a room and just look good. But when a *sexy* man walks in a room, women can be with their man and they still look, and gonna grunt and whisper and all that. So, trust me when I tell you this. You have both qualities."

Daquan stood up and towered over Asia. "At this point, I'm with whatever..." he said, "...set it up."

Asia flashed a smile, walked around and reached for her

phone. And as she was picking it up, it was ringing. She swiped the green button. "Hello."

"Hello, someone called me from this number," a female's voice asked from the other end.

Asia gave a confused look. She knew she hadn't called anybody from her phone except for her dad. She didn't recall it. "I'm sorry, I didn't," Asia said, then she asked, "Was the call made today?"

"No, it was yesterday."

Asia looked at Daquan. "Did you call anybody form my phone yesterday?"

Daquan thought about it for a second, his head was slightly cocked to the right. Then he snapped his fingers. "Yeah." He reached for the phone.

Daquan received the phone. "Hello, is this the lady about renting out the basement?"

"Yes, it is," she replied.

"Yes ma'am, I'm Daquan, my fiancée and me was interested, but I just lost my job today, so I'm going to have to pass on it."

"Okay, sorry to hear that. What kind of work do you do?" she asked him.

Daquan paused for a moment. "I can do anything, cut grass, cut trees, lay bricks, paint."

"What about plumbing work," she asked him.

Plumbing? He thought about the trade that he took while he was in prison. "Yes ma'am, I can do that," he responded.

"Okay, when will be a good time you and your fiancée can come out and look at the basement?"

Daquan looked at Asia. She nodded and moved her lips. "Now," she whispered. He said back into the phone. "We'll call an Uber and we can be there in less than an hour, depending on traffic."

"Okay, great. See you guys when you get here." She hung up.

Daquan looked at Asia and she was looking at him as well. "What you think," he asked her.

"Sounds like God is working in our favor," Asia responded, her lips curled up. She hugged Daquan and he wrapped his arms around her and drew her in to him.

CHAPTER 15

*A*sia and Daquan had the Uber driver pull up in the driveway of an old Victorian style house somewhere in Midtown Atlanta. Daquan got out of the rear driver side door and Asia slid over and got out behind him. He then leaned down and looked at the driver. "Thanks a lot." He closed the door and the driver backed out of the driveway. He turned around and grabbed Asia by the hand, and they walked up a winding concrete walkway that took them to the front door. The front porch was screened in. Daquan knocked on the screen door.

"Who is it," a voice asked from behind the door.

"It's Daquan, I just spoke with you over the phone about the basement rental."

The front door came open. A short pale lady that looked to be at least eighty years old came onto the front porch and unlocked the screen door. She looked at Daquan and Asia. She hesitated for a moment, but then moved to the side. "Y'all can come on in," the old lady said.

Daquan allowed Asia to go in onto the front porch first, walking in behind her. Asia put her hand out to the lady. "I'm Asia."

The old lady had small wrinkled hands and gave her hand to Asia. "Nice to meet you, Asia. Was you the young lady that answered the phone?"

"Yes ma'am, I am."

"Good, my name is Elizabeth." She then looked over at Daquan, "...and you must be the young man that just lost his job."

Daquan smiled, even though the sound of that was uncomfortable. "Yes ma'am." He gave her his hand and they shook hands.

"Follow me." She turned and went through the threshold into the living room. The inside of the house looked as if they'd just entered into another world. Everything was antique, from the floors, the furniture and the ceilings. Elizabeth escorted them over to a lavender and gold loveseat. "Y'all can have a seat."

Asia and Daquan sat down next to one another and she sat in a matching chair next to them. Elizabeth was an eighty-two-year-old white lady that had been living in mid-town Atlanta in the same house for the last thirty-nine years. She had a lot of history in that house, and in the city as well. She finally turned her attention to Daquan and Asia.

"I don't have a basement for rent."

The silence set in throughout the house. Daquan had his eyes glued to the old lady, then she said. "Not for the both of you anyway." She paused, took a breath. "How long do y'all plan on staying?"

"You just said..."

Asia nudged Daquan, cutting him off from what he was about to say. "We're just looking for somewhere for a few months until we get on our feet, our baby will arrive in about six months."

Elizabeth smiled and flashed a mouth full of dentures. "It's a baby coming? What a blessing, child."

"Yes ma'am, thank you."

The old lady sat in silence again, looking at Daquan. "I'm gonna need somebody to keep the house fixed up around here. My late husband Richard died last year. Fifty-eight years we were married." She paused and dropped her head in silence for a brief moment. She finally looked back up. "I just don't want to stay here by myself. If you can maintain the property, you'll can stay here rent free, it's a two-bedroom guesthouse out back. Now, my Richard use to keep it up cause his parents used to come in from Valdosta, Georgia, every other month until they died. But it may need some painting and cleaning and whatever." She paused and took yet another breathe, then she touched her chest. "Excuse me, I can't talk long like I used to."

Asia was nearly in tears. She blurted out, "So, you're saying that we can stay in the guest house out back as long as we want? As long as we keep the maintenance up on the property?"

Elizabeth nodded her head up and down. "I got one grandson, and he lives all the way up in Toronto, Canada. He wants to get me up there so I can stay in an old folks' home. I'm not going." Then she pushed herself up from the chair. "Let me show y'all the guest house." She started walking toward the back of the house, leading them down a long wooden hallway that took them to the kitchen. She unlocked the door, walked out on the back porch, which was also screened in like the front porch. Asia and Daquan walked out on the porch and stopped when she did. "I don't like to go up and down the steps right there." She pointed at the steps that led down to the backyard. "But that's it." She pointed toward the house. It was made of white brick and looked to be more than two bedrooms. There were two rocking chairs on the front porch, and a wide spacious yard with high grass that was desperately in need of a cut.

"Can we go take a look on the inside?" Daquan asked with excitement in his voice.

Elizabeth turned around and went toward the door that led back to the kitchen. "Let me get the key." She opened the door, kept it propped open with her leg as if she was retrieving the keys from a stub on the wall. Elizabeth turned back around, handed the keys to Daquan. "The alarm code is one, two, three, four," she said and held up her fingers as she said it.

Asia opened the screen door first and walked down the steps, they were a little unstable. Daquan went down behind her, and they walked across the huge yard side by side. "I don't believe this," Asia whispered.

Daquan kept walking; he was quiet and in thought. When they reached the front porch of the house, he slid the key inside the lock and turned it. The alarm chimed; the pad was right next to the door. He turned on the lights and disarmed the ADT alarm. The living room was spacious; there was a three-piece furniture set that was covered with blankets. The place smelled a little stale, but that wouldn't be a problem. He wiped down a few cobwebs with his hands as he walked over toward the dining room table. The kitchen was just behind the dining room area. Asia flipped on the light switch and walked into the kitchen. It was spacious with an island stove, granite counter tops and wooden cabinets, a white refrigerator, and dishwasher. The sink overlooked the backyard that had a privacy fence. "This shit is nice," Daquan said to Asia.

She turned to him, her eyes were filled with joy. "Let's go see the bedrooms." She walked past Daquan and he followed closely behind her. They went out the kitchen and around the corner, down a short hallway. There was a bathroom to their left. Daquan stopped and opened the door, flipping the switch, but the bulb was blown. There was a tub and a shower, a toilet, and sink. He pulled the door closed and went on down the hall behind Asia. He looked in the room to his left and saw how spacious it was. There wasn't a bed, but there was a mattress leaning up against the wall. Asia was in the bathroom.

"Man, you got to see this," she called out.

Daquan walked over to where the bathroom was. When he

got to the door, he couldn't believe it. There were a his and hers sink, a glass wall standup shower with white marble looking tile. And there was an oval shaped Jacuzzi tub with jets that separated both of the sinks. Seeing another door, Daquan turned the knob, opened it, and came into a spacious walk-in closet that was big enough for the both of them.

"I still can't believe this," Asia whispered.

"Believe it," Daquan said, and hugged her tight. "All we got to do is believe, and we can achieve it."

THEY FINALLY WALKED OUT AND WENT BACK TO THE MAIN HOUSE. The old lady was sitting in her rocking chair when they walked up the stairs and opened the door. Asia walked through the door first and she had a wide bright smile on her face.

"Y'all like it?" Elizabeth asked them.

"We love it," Asia said.

Then Daquan said, "Yes ma'am, it's nice." He walked up to her, leaned down and took her hand and held it. "You just don't know how much this means to us," he told her in a heart-warming tone. "And I know you said just keep the maintenance up, but are you sure that we can't pay you at least five hundred dollars a month?"

Elizabeth had crowfeet wrinkles around her eyes and mouth, her hair was nearly silver, and she wore it in a ponytail. When her hand squeezed his, she whispered, "Let me think about it."

He smiled, shook his head, and then looked back at Asia. "She funny."

Asia softly clapped her hands together with joy. "Miss Elizabeth, when can we move in?"

"You got the keys. Soon as you want."

Asia walked over to her and wrapped her arms around her neck. Asia hugged her and broke out in tears. "Thank you so much." She barely got her words out when the old lady stood up; she wasn't in too bad of shape for her age. She and Asia were about the same height.

"Oh, you're welcome darling," she responded back and clapped Asia softly on her back. When she pulled away from her, she looked her in her eyes and then scanned her up and down. "What kind of work do you do?"

"I'm a waitress at a restaurant, Yard House in Atlantic Station."

"That's where you plan on retiring from?" Elizabeth asked her.

"Oh, no ma'am. I just needed something that was going to bring us an income. I've only been there a few days. We were staying in a motel until this came about."

The old lady listened, her ears were still good; she moved her head up and down, then she turned around, grabbed the door handle. "Come on, let's go inside."

Daquan moved around and held the door for her as she walked in, Asia went in next. Daquan followed behind them, making sure to lock the door. She stopped in the kitchen, opened the fridge, and pulled out a plastic green pitcher of sweet tea and sat it on the counter. "Sweet tea, which I don't drank. I used to make a jug every three days for my Richard." She went to the sink and poured it out. Then she looked at them. "When are y'all two getting married?"

They looked at one another, both smiling. Then Daquan said, "We don't have an official date, but we were planning on just going to the courthouse and getting it done once we got ourselves situated."

"That's a blessing within itself." Then she paused and got quiet for a moment, her body relaxed. "I'm not going to talk you two ears off today, it's getting late, and I try to be in the bed at seven every evening and up at six in the morning." She turned toward Daquan, pointing her finger at him. "Tool shed out back, everything you need should be there. The garage is on the side, it has the riding mower and paint. You'll see."

Daquan nodded. "Yes ma'am. I'll be sure to get here bright and early to get situated."

* * *

WINTERTIME HAD ARRIVED IN ATLANTA, AND IT WAS A WEEK before Thanksgiving and Asia stomach was plumped. She was sitting on the sofa watching a show on Netflix. Daquan had fixed up their house to the point where they both agreed upon. They had a nice flat screen smart TV mounted on the wall just above the fireplace. The floors were covered with a cream-colored carpet, and they'd kept the same furniture that was already there. It was nine o' seven at night when she heard Daquan coming through the door. When he walked in, he was carrying a few plastic grocery bags from Publix. He locked the door, turned and went straight to Asia. She sat up. "Hey baby." She smiled at him.

Daquan bent over and kissed her lips. "How you feelin'," he asked her. There were three grocery bags all together, the one that he had for her was all the junk food that she requested. He gave her the bag and as she took it, she said, "I'm feeling pretty good, just been tired or lazy."

"Let's say tired." He began walking into the kitchen with the bags. Once he put his muscle milk and vitamins up, he walked back into the living room where Asia was just about to open up her bag of Doritos. Daquan got in front of her, dropped down to one knee, and produced a diamond ring so big that it looked fake. He didn't have it in a box, he was just holding it between his thumb and index finger. Asia dropped the bag of chips while she was staring at the ring. "My God, yes!" she said anxiously.

"Damn! At least let me ask you first," Daquan said with a smile.

"Okay, ask me." Asia began jumping up and down on the sofa like a kid in a candy store.

"Will you be my wife forever, like Miss Elizabeth and Richard was?"

Asia smiled and covered her face. She was filled with so much joy that she nearly jumped in Daquan's arms. "Yes baby. Couple goals."

"Jay Z and Beyoncé?" he asked, smiling as he began sliding the ring on her finger.

"Michelle and Barack?" She held it up and looked at it.

"Bonnie and Clyde?" Daquan kissed her.

"Russell and Ciara?" she said to him between kisses.

"I'm a Future fan," Daquan said and laughed.

Asia playfully punched him as they hugged and held each other.

"What?" He laughed even harder. "What about Ike and Tina?"

"Boy, you going a little too far now. Last one. Nipsey and Lauren?"

Daquan squeezed Asia even tighter. They kissed for the next three to four minutes, just enjoying the moment. Then he whispered in Asia's ear, "Last one for real." He paused, and then went on. "Kobe and Vanessa?" At that moment, they held on to one another; she had her head resting on Daquan's shoulder as tears of joy streamed down her cheeks. "I don't never want to be without you. I love you, Daquan."

"I love you too, Asia," he whispered, then he reached and wiped away the tears that had began to form in his eyes.

Asia looked up at him. She was in tears, and then she smiled. "It's okay to cry. At least we're happy."

EPILOGUE

*A*sia had on a white wedding gown with all the fancy bells and whistles, and her hair was made up perfectly by one of the best hairstylists in Atlanta. Daquan wanted to wear some jeans and Polo shirt. However, Miss Elizabeth wasn't having it. That day he was dressed in a black and white tailor-made tuxedo, a bowtie, and hard bottom shoes. When Asia walked out of the Fulton County courthouse, Daquan was right there with her, just as happy as could be.

"Stop right there, let me get a picture," said Asia's mother, standing on the steps a few feet below them. She and Asia had settled their differences; even though her father didn't make it, he still called and Facetimed her and Daquan. Most of the time, fathers can be rough when it comes to their daughters. He actually had a good conversation with Daquan and took a liking to him. After the pictures were taken, they went out to eat, Asia, Daquan, Miss Elizabeth, and Asia's mother.

THE BABY ARRIVED A FEW MONTHS LATER; IT WAS A LITTLE GIRL and she was adorable. They named her Angel, and Daquan fell in love with her at first sight—he had his wife and child. And Asia had her husband and her healthy baby.

Two months after Angel was born, Asia got a call from the Mexican lady that her and Daquan had met on the Greyhound bus. That day, the lady asked if her and Daquan could meet them in the parking lot of a Best Buy in Alpharetta. When they arrived, the Mexican lady's husband was there. He thanked Daquan and Asia for everything and then he gave them a Best Buy bag with a box on the inside. "Your reward," the Mexican said to him. Then he hugged him. "Thank you."

"Thank you, mi amigo."

When they got home, they opened the box that displayed a MacBook Pro on it. It was fifty thousand dollars in cash, all one hundred-dollar bills, and a note that read: **If you ever need me for anything, call my wife's number. Thank you again.**

FROM THERE, ASIA AND DAQUAN STARTED THEIR OWN BUSINESS, A barber, nail, and eyelash shop in the heart of Midtown, Atlanta, and it flourished because Daquan had a huge following from his Instagram page.

ALMOST THE END

*H*ey ladies, this me again. I'm a little more grown up now. Who in the world would've thought that I had to go through something like this cause I was tryna be somebody wife? Like honestly, I just wanted to share that part with y'all. It hurt like hell to know that dog Angelo...You know what, I'm not gonna even call him out his name. Just know that he's down there in Houston still doing the same old thing. I actually got a little nosey and reached out to his sister, Kat, and she spilled the beans. How about she started being the Mule for her brother. Yeah, she said she got caught with a lot of his money and when the police asked her where she got it from, she told them it was her brother's money. Now he's under Federal investigation and they took all his houses, cars and a few businesses. All I said was to her was: Umph, God put his hands on him.

BUT FRIEND, LET ME TELL Y'ALL THIS. CRAZY MAN SEAN CAUGHT thirty years. That's right, he went to prison. But the trip part is that Nu Nu tried to go be a correctional officer at the same prison he was at, and as soon as she got in her cadet uniform, she got busted bringing Sean some Meth and a cellphone. They locked lil ugly ass right up. And as I'm typing this, I'm just sitting here on my front porch sipping some green tea with Miss. Elizabeth, she told me tell everyone hello and she's doing just fine.

I'm doing fine too, y'all. I finally got what I wanted and more. I'm somebody's wife, I'm a mom, I'm happy, and most important of all, I'm loved by an awesome man.

AUTHOR NOTE

If I said that I didn't enjoy writing this book, I'd be lying. So, when I actually came up with this plot, it wasn't anything how it ended. And my reason for changing it up was because I wanted to touch on a few topics about love, life and relationship goals. Now let me see, where will I start?

SINGLE:

MARRIED:

WE JUST GO TOGETHER:

OPEN RELATIONSHIP:

In some form or fashion, you've been through one of the above. Now I know in some elements of the book, Asia was dumb, smart, naïve, and in love. Just as, well, every one of you have been at some point in your life. And that's alright, because EVERYONE has been in a relationship with that one dude that made you think that all men were the same. Some of you left, moved on, and got into a better situation, some got into a WORSER situation. And I know *worser* isn't a word. But somebody that's reading this right now has said it at least one time. Take the guy Sean for example. If you'd just left a relationship and met a HIM, I would love to hear about it in your review when you leave it. And it's simple, if you met a Sean, an Angelo, or a Daquan, not just the names, but someone similar to one of these characters, I'd like to hear your story, that's if you would like to share it. You can **email me: mrhart35@gmail.com** or you can message me on my personal **Facebook page: Jarvis Cole Hart Hardwick or my fanpage: Author Cole Hart. Twitter page: Author Cole Hart. IG: Author Cole Hart.** When you send me your story, just a letter now, not no five thousand words or nothing like that. Lol. Let me know if you don't mind me sharing it with the rest of the readers, fans, and supporters because I will be selecting some to be entered into my giveaway contest that'll be hosted in my Facebook readers group. If you do wish to participate in the contests/giveaways, please be sure to join the group: Cole Hart Signature Readers Club on Facebook, so you won't miss your name and/or letter being announced.

And let me give a *special shout out* to my homegirl that gave me her story and asked me to write it. You know who you are because it's dedicated to EVERY WOMAN around the world that had to go through something terrible in life to get to something great, wonderful, and loving. And ladies, just because you ask for something or someone in particular and it don't come when you want it or how you want, doesn't mean that it's not coming. You must continue to see your vision, see your dream. Speak it every day as if you already have it. If you stop visualizing it, it will disappear. So regardless, if it's the big home you want, see yourself in that particular home cooking dinner in your gourmet kitchen for you and your family. Hold that vision if that's what you desire. If it's a particular car that you desire, see yourself walking out into your garage and pressing the alarm on that particular car, get in, see the Mercedes, Bentley, RR emblem in the center of the steering wheel. Smell the leather, feel the leather. Put your favorite song on, check your hair in the mirror, see if your lips are popping, your eyelashes like you want them. *This* is how you **hold** the vision. If it's a certain type of man you want. Same way, you want him tall, chocolate and a six-pack, or short and chubby like me. Lol. Either way, your dreams and goals are yours. Keep praying, stay focused. God first always. With my hands pressed together, I am sending up a massive prayer for all of us as we go through this rough time with this Corona ordeal. So many families have been affected by this, and I'm praying every day for us as a whole.

Well, until we meet at a book signing, stay blessed and thank you for your ongoing support. And don't forget. Leave your review. I love to hear what you like and don't like about the story.

PS. Never give up and always keep God first.

CPSIA information can be obtained
at www.ICGtesting.com
Printed in the USA
LVHW030157090721
692195LV00005B/681